# CLAY BRENTWOOD BOOK TWO:
# UNJUST PUNISHMENT

Creative Texts Publishers products are available at special discounts for bulk purchase for sale promotions, premiums, fund-raising, and educational needs. For details, write Creative Texts Publishers, PO Box 50, Barto, PA 19504, or visit www.creativetexts.com

CLAY BRENTWOOD: BOOK TWO: UNJUST PUNISHMENT
by Jared McVay
Published by Creative Texts Publishers
PO Box 50
Barto, PA 19504
www.creativetexts.com



ISBN: 9780692166307

CLAY BRENTWOOD™

# UNJUST PUNISHMENT

By

JARED MCVAY

SIX GUN BOOKS™

An imprint of Creative Texts Publishers, LLC
Barto, PA

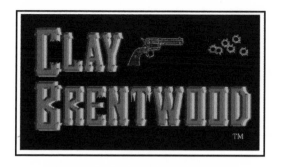

This book is dedicated to
western fans across
the world

Thank you one and all. It’s for you
I write.
[and of course, for me too]

## AUTHOR'S NOTE

In every work of fiction, the reader may see something or someone who seems familiar, but if that happens in my story, it's just because my leprechaun is messing with you.

Jared

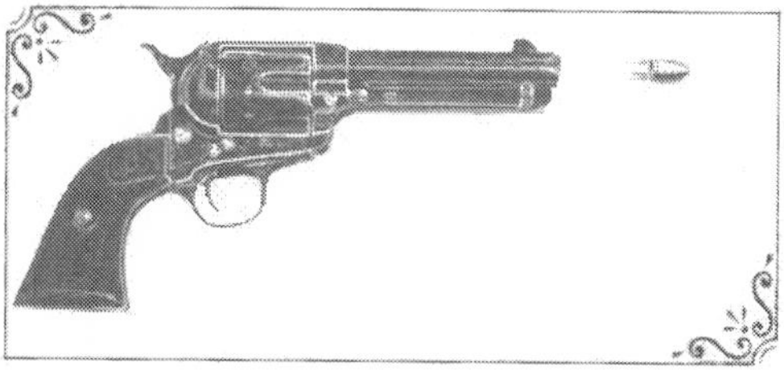

# CHAPTER ONE

-

Between Albuquerque and Bristol Springs, the land was not much but dry desert, cacti, snakes, and scorpions. This was an ancient land where little had changed over the past million years or so. Life was harsh, and only the strong survived.

Scattered around were hidden valleys with trees and lush grass, and even water. In other places the lifesaving liquid seeped from the rocks with enough to save a man's life, but you had to know where to look, or get lucky in finding it. Many fleeing outlaws, along with prospectors and greenhorns died here, sometimes just a few feet from the lifesaving liquid.

Astride the black stallion, Clay Brentwood rode south across this desolate no-mans land, his eyes unconsciously scanning places where trouble might show up in the form of Indians or bandits. During the past several years, trouble had followed him like a shadow and he was still alive because he watched and listened for anything out of the ordinary, like the sun glancing off metal, a scuffed stone, or the sound of a hammer on a gun being cocked; even the sound of a rattlesnake whose path he might be crossing.

As Clay rode along, his troubled mind searched for answers. Was it finally over he wondered as he pulled down the wide brim of his Texas hat to shade his eyes from the scorching sun and still allow him to keep a constant surveillance on the area ahead; or would trouble follow him wherever he went? Would there be more killing? He hoped not; he'd had enough to last a lifetime – more than most men would ever know.

Sweat ran down into his eyes and made them burn. His sun baked shirt felt hot against his skin. Every joint in his body ached, and suddenly at the age of thirty-two, the past four years seemed to be catching up with him and he felt old and bone weary.

At heart, he had always been a quiet, peaceful man – a rancher, or used to be, with a wife and child on the way. But when the unscrupulous Curly Beeler and his gang of cutthroats attacked his ranch and shot him in the head, then raped and murdered his wife, Martha, everything changed. They burned the house, barn, and outbuildings to the ground. They stole his horses and cattle. But none of that mattered, it could all be replaced – but nothing could replace his wife, or the child she was carrying. They were lost to him, forever. And for that, Curly Beeler and his gang of miscreants had to pay with their lives. This he had sworn, with tears running from his eyes, as he knelt next to her grave.

Avenging her death became an obsession with him. For two and a half years they eluded him until he finally caught up with them in the small town of Bristol Springs in the lower part of the New Mexico Territory. Here, in this small town, his chase ended and his reputation as a gunfighter began. Bold as brass, he'd ridden the black stallion into town, executed the men who'd murdered his wife, and then without a word, he got back on the black stallion and rode out of town.

After avenging his wife's death by killing Curly and his gang, he tried to escape being thought of as a gunfighter by taking the job of Segundo on Senora Ontiveros' ranchero. Gunfights with cattle rustlers from across the border, along with a face-to-face shootout with two no-good white men he'd fired from the senora's payroll, only fed fuel to his gunfighters' image.

If that hadn't been enough, a few months ago, slavers kidnapped his boss, Senora Ontiveros, along with twelve other women, intending to take them down into Mexico where they would be sold as slaves and prostitutes.

After three months of trailing the slavers, and almost dying in the desert from lack of food and water, he finally caught up with them. With the help of a ten-year-old Indian boy he met along the way, they rescued the women. The slavers got their just reward in front of a firing squad made up of twelve women - and a ten-year-old Indian boy.

At the request of the senora, he'd seen to it that all the women got back to their homes safely. And when at last, in Albuquerque, he'd put the last two women and the Indian boy on a train back to California, Clay headed back down to the ranchero to tell the senora he would be returning to his ranch in Texas. He knew she would not like the idea, but it was time for him to hang up his gun and go home. He needed to rebuild and start over. He wanted to work his own land – raise his own cattle and horses.

Because of an inheritance left to him by his late wife and her father, he was a wealthy man with several lucrative businesses back in Wichita, Kansas, still bringing in money. He owned several thousand acres of good grass in the heartland of Texas that had plenty of water for the cattle and horses he wanted to raise.

He lit a store-bought cigarillo he'd purchased before leaving Albuquerque and blew smoke into the air, allowing his body to relax for the first time in a long while. It was finally settled in his mind. He was going home and he was happy about his decision. He knew his dead wife, Martha, would also be happy about his decision.

He was sure the senora had ideas where he was concerned. She'd been subtle, but he'd caught her drift on several occasions. She was beautiful, rich and owned a big chunk of the New Mexico Territory, but the idea of another wife, even as beautiful and rich as the senora, was not one of his priorities. Maybe someday, if it was supposed to happen, but he wouldn't push the idea.

Suddenly, he felt as though a weight had been lifted from his shoulders and he lifted his voice in song.

Clay didn't have what a person might call a great singing voice, but that didn't matter, it made him feel good, and right now, that was what counted.

A buzzard circled high overhead, curious about the loud noise coming from the desert floor, and then flew away when a coyote raised his head and joined the off-key singing.

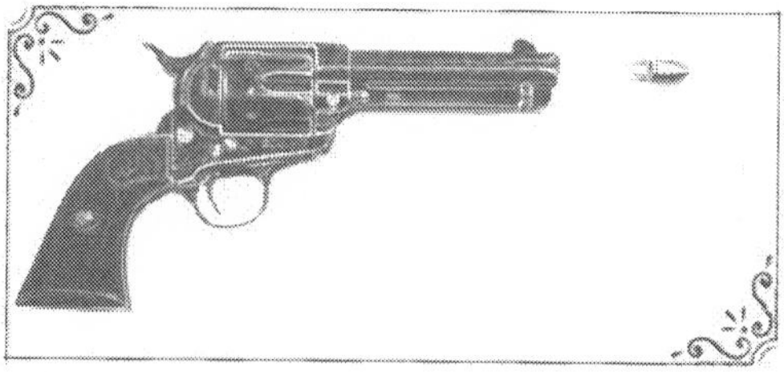

# CHAPTER TWO

The late afternoon sun was creeping toward the distant horizon as the black stallion reached the crest of the steep hill and stopped to blow. Like his master, he too had almost died in the desert from lack of food, water, and heat. Only his loyalty to the man on his back had kept him on his feet.

As he stood there catching his wind, he sensed the change in the man on his back, which also allowed him to relax.

During the past four years, they had crossed the river and gone over a mountain or two, and he had come to enjoy the feel of the man on his back.

Clay reached down and patted the big horse on the neck and said, “It’s alright big fella, just ah little ways more and we can both get some food and rest.”

The big horse nodded its head up and down as if he understood, then headed down the hill.

The smell of fresh hay filling his nostrils made the black stallion anxious to get to the stable as he high-stepped his way down the main street.

People stopped to stare and wave as Clay passed by.

Keeping his right hand not far from the forty-four pistol on his hip, a habit he'd gotten into during the last several years, Clay put two fingers of his left hand to the brim of his hat in acknowledgement to their greetings.

To the people of Bristol Springs, Clay Brentwood would forever be a hero. Not only had he cleaned up the Beeler gang, single-handed, but had also rid the town of Frank Cushin and Harley Grimm, two bullies who had terrorized the citizenship of their small community off and on for several years.

Clay had almost ridden on, bypassing Bristol Springs. They were good people, one and all, but their admiration for him was ah mite hard to take.

In the end, because it was late and both he and his horse were tired and hungry, he figured he could endure their kindness one more time before going back to Texas.

Nathan, the owner of the livery stable, seemed happy to see them and promised to take good care of the black stallion, while the owner of the saloon was more than happy to provide Clay with a supper of steak, fried potatoes, pinto beans, cornbread and two mugs of cold beer. Nothing was too good for the man who had killed Curly Beeler, right here in his saloon. People from all over were still coming to see the blood-stained floor where Curly had died and to listen to him tell the story, which got a bit more exciting each time it was told.

At the barbershop, Clay was treated to a haircut, a shave, a bath, and clean clothes.

Even his hotel room was gratis.

After he'd shucked down and climbed into bed, his eyes had no more than closed when the sound of heavy snoring filled the room.

That night, he dreamed of being on his ranch, herding cattle and rounding up wild horses to break - of coming home at the end of the day to a wife and child; of sitting on the porch after supper, playing a guitar and enjoying the sunset. He smiled in his sleep because he didn't know how to play a guitar.

Such were the way of dreams. At least for this one night, he was at peace – but… the fickle finger of fate had other ideas about

Clay Brentwood's future where his dreams would not be so pleasant.

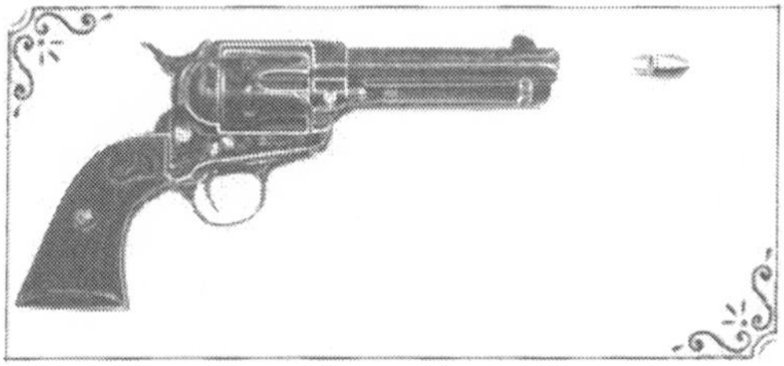

# CHAPTER THREE

-

Captain Bill McDaniel, head of the infamous Texas Rangers, was a man with a long-standing reputation. He'd never gone after a man he didn't bring back, one way or another. Upright or laying face down over the saddle, it was all the same to him. He actually preferred them face down, they were less troublesome that way.

McDaniel enjoyed his reputation, and because of it, his own men walked lightly in his presence, and bad men sometimes just gave up, figuring prison was better than being shot.

And now, he was on the trail of a man called Clay Brentwood. He'd just missed him in Albuquerque, but after riding all night he topped over a hill shortly after daylight and saw a small town in front of him. His skin began to tighten and he got the feeling he was getting close to the end of his chase.

Tired and hungry, the light in the window of the restaurant beckoned him, and after seeing his horse taken care of, Bill headed for the only eating-house in town, figuring he could pick up some information there.

Standing just inside the doorway, he took in the aroma of freshly made apple pie while his eyes roamed over the people seated at the counter and tables. None of the men resembled the description he carried in his vest pocket, and after a moment, he headed toward a table at the back of the room where he could watch the front door.

One of the men recognized Bill McDaniel from a picture he'd seen in the paper, and knowing of the man's reputation, quickly spread the word to the other customers; all of them wondering why he was in town - hoping he was just passing through.

Bill heard the whispers and smiled. They knew of him, which meant they would stay out of the way, if and when it came time for lead to fly.

After ordering the four-bit special, which included a piece of apple pie, Bill settled back with the cup of coffee the waitress had brought him and listened to whispered conversations. The one that caught his attention was two ladies speaking about the very man he was looking for - except, they were talking about him as though he was some kind of hero instead of a low down, cold blooded murderer.

When the waitress brought his food, he asked her, “Do you know this Clay Brentwood everyone seems to be talking about? Does he live here in Bristol Springs?”

The waitress, a woman in her mid-forties, large of structure, with a wide grin that was filled with teeth, looked as though she was about to blush. “Oh my, heavens no, he don’t live here, but most of the town wishes he did. I guess nobody here in town knows him very well. He just rode into town one day and saved it from the Beeler gang, and then rode out. And the next time he came in, he shot it out with Frank Cushin, a no-good who had been terrorizing folks around here for some time, and the strange thing was, Mister Brentwood was blind as a bat at the time; with bandages over his eyes. Frank Cushin called him out, and he out-drew and shot Frank down just like he could see him. It was uncanny, I tell you - uncanny!”

Bill could see her face getting flushed. It made no sense. Surely, this couldn’t be the same man he was looking for. And what was this about the man being blind? How did he…? His thoughts were interrupted when she continued.

"We found out he went to work for Senora Ontiveros on her ranchero south of town. He's her Segundo. You know, foreman. He got rock splinters in his eyes while he was shooting it out with some Mexican bandits and had his eyes all bandaged up when Frank called him out - but he's alright now."

"So, he's not here in town?"

"I didn't say that," the waitress said, smoothing out her gray hair. "He rode into town last night and spent the night at the hotel. If you're in a big hurry to talk to him, he might still be there. But my guess is, he'll be coming through the door most any time, wanting his breakfast before he rides on down to the senora's ranchero."

Bill McDaniel nodded his head and dug into his breakfast of biscuits, gravy, three eggs, a steak and fried potatoes. He would let his prey come to him. He was in no hurry. Besides, he had that piece of apple pie to look forward to.

The more Bill listened, the more confused he became. Judge Horatio B. Tyson had described Clay Brentwood as a hardened criminal who killed innocent folks just for the sport of it – a man with no conscience. He'd warned Bill to ride with both eyes open and maybe consider the old adage, shoot first and ask questions later.

The bell over the door warned of someone coming in and Bill looked up. The hair on the back of his neck stood on end and his hand dropped for the pistol on his hip. His man was standing there, just a few feet away, easy for the taking. He could call out his name and when Clay looked at him he could shoot, claiming he thought the man was going for his gun.

But for some reason, he stayed his hand. People were walking up to him and shaking his hand and patting him on the back.

Taking a mouthful of biscuits and gravy, Bill decided to let things ride for a bit. Hadn't the waitress said this man was hell on wheels with a gun? He hadn't lived this long by rushing into situations he wasn't in control of. Besides, to shoot it out here in the restaurant might get some innocent folks hurt, or even killed, and Judge Tyson wouldn't cotton to that.

The waitress was already there with a mug of coffee when Clay sat down at the counter. "Breakfast coming right up," she said with a big smile, then mentioned that the man at the back table was looking for him.

Bill McDaniel had just stabbed a piece of steak when a shadow fell across his plate. He looked up and found himself looking into the face of Clay Brentwood.

"Barbara Jean, the waitress, said you're lookin' ta talk ta me."

Bill nodded toward the chair opposite him and said, "Please, have a seat. You're welcome to have your breakfast here, with me. And yes, we do need to talk."

Clay pulled the chair back and sat down, his right hand never far from the gun on his hip, which didn't go unnoticed by McDaniel.

The waitress brought his coffee over and asked, "You eating breakfast, here?"

Clay accepted the coffee and nodded his head. When Barbara Jean was gone, he turned his attention back to the man across the table from him, noticing the man's right hand was out of sight and possibly inside his coat where he might have a hideout gun. Many men out here seemed to be doin' that, lately.

Clay didn't know this man or why he wanted to talk to him, but as long as they were this close, he didn't figure the man would be stupid enough to start something here in the restaurant.

"Now then, what do we need ta talk about?" Clay asked in a casual tone. Using his left hand, he took a sip of coffee. It never hurt to stay cautious.

McDaniel took his time and swallowed the mouthful of food he'd been chewing. After a sip of coffee, he said, "McDaniel, Bill McDaniel. Mean anything to you?"

"Heard of ah man named McDaniel; captain or something – with the Texas Rangers. Can't say I've ever met the man. So, what's he got to do with me?"

"I'm Captain McDaniel, and you are Clay Brentwood. Right?"

At that moment, Barbara Jean brought Clay's breakfast and re-filled their coffee cups.

"Are you ready for your pie?" she asked of Bill, who shook his head. "I'll wait and eat my pie when Mister Brentwood eats his."

When Barbara Jean was gone, Clay said, "Yes, my name is Brentwood. Now what's this all about? If the rangers are tryin' to recruit me..."

Bill held up his hand, deciding he'd better just come out with it and see how the cards fell. "I've come to arrest you and take you back to Texas. I have two warrants for your arrest – one for the murder of Charles "Curly" Beeler, and the other for a man up in Kansas by the name of, Revers Milan."

This was a tense moment and Bill McDaniel held himself ready, watching the man's eyes, and was surprised by Clay's reaction.

"I don't know anybody by the name of Revers Milan," Clay said. "And as far as Curly Beeler goes, he had it comin'."

McDaniel studied the man across the table from him and didn't know what to think. This was not the way he'd pictured it going down. The man was totally different from what he'd expected him to be.

"Not for me to say, one way or another. I'm just the man they sent to bring you in. It will be up to the judge to decide whether you're innocent or guilty. Now, I'm hoping we can do this the easy way. As to trading lead at this range, neither of us would miss."

Clay relaxed and gave out with a chuckle. "Mister, I ain't no fool, and I don't go out of my way lookin' for trouble. There's too much of it comes huntin' me as it is. How about I finish my breakfast, then you and me take a walk so's we can hash this over in private. I'm not the gunman you seem to think I am. When ya get right down to it, I reckon I'm just ah peace lovin' fella who wants nuthin' more than to be ah rancher, and if the good Lord is willin', ah family man."

Bill McDaniel glanced around the room and saw several men with hands close to their weapons, ready to side with this man if it came to that.

"Sure," Bill said. "We can do that. Besides I'm kind of looking forward to that pie. Been awhile since I've had any."

Standing with their elbows resting on the top rail of the corral, Clay told McDaniel the story behind Curly Beeler and his gang, leaving nothing out. And when he'd finished, he shook his head and said, "Now, as for that Milan fella, I've been searchin' my brain and I'll swear, I've never laid eyes on anybody by that name – up in Kansas, down in Texas, or anywhere else."

McDaniel filled his jaw with chew and worried it a bit, then spit a stream of brown juice into the corral. "I'll swan, this sure ain't turning out like I thought it would."

"What's that mean?" Clay asked.

McDaniel spit another stream of juice and wiped his chin. "It means I'm inclined to believe you son, but that don't mean a hill of beans. I got paper on you. It's my sworn duty to take you into custody and take you back to Texas to stand trial."

Knowin' if he didn't go back with the ranger and get this cleared up; he could never go back to Texas, ever again. "And if I elect ta not go back?" he asked in a casual manner.

Bill McDaniel stepped back and pushed his coat aside. "Then we have at it, here and now. What's it going to be?"

Clay grinned and raised his hands. "Okay, you win. The last thing I need is to have the death of a Texas Ranger on my hands. Especially, a famous one like you."

Bill McDaniel let out a sigh of relief. From what he'd heard, he wasn't sure he could out draw this man who claimed to not be a gunfighter. The man had put at least twelve men that he knew of, face up in boot hill. "You mean that? You'll mind your manners all the way back to Texas?"

"I will," Clay said, "But I'll be hirin' ah mouthpiece as soon as we get there, and in the meantime, I need ta tell my boss I'm leavin'. Wouldn't want ta leave her in ah lurch."

As they rode south out of Bristol Springs, Nathan, who had been standing in the shadow of the barn and had heard everything, soon spread the story all over town.

Within half an hour, there wasn't a man, woman, or child who didn't know Clay had been arrested for the murder of Curly Beeler.

"By Gawd," Ned Baker, owner of the mercantile store, said, his booming voice rattling the windowpanes. "Somebody needs to go to Texas and tell that judge ah thing or two!"

There wasn't a person in town who didn't agree with Ned, but two things stopped them. First, was the cost of the trip - none of them had that kind of extra money. And the second was, no one knew where in Texas the ranger would be taking him.

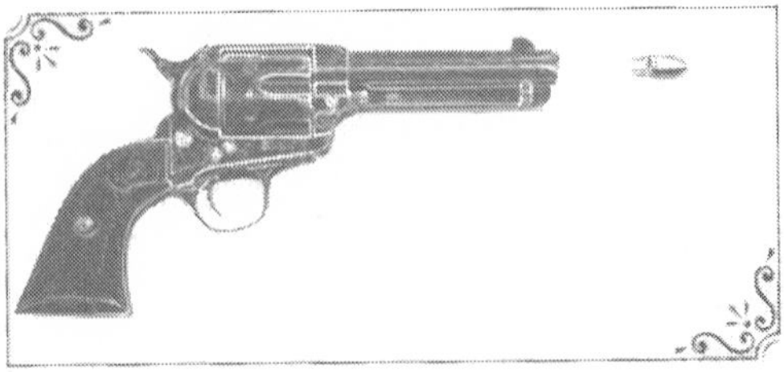

# CHAPTER FOUR

-

The senora did not take the news well and vowed to go to Texas and speak to the judge. But after a lot of persuasion by Clay, telling her there was no need for worry, she relented, assuring him there would always be a place for him on her ranchero, should he decide to come back. Clay didn't see the tears run down the senora's cheeks as they rode away.

After three long days on the trail, they stood on the platform at the train station in Albuquerque where they bought tickets to Austin along with passage for their horses. They reasoned that riding all that way on horseback would take several weeks, and would be hard on both, them and the horses. Taking the train made more sense. Besides, it would be a lot more comfortable. The train had beds, a dining car and a bar. They'd have nothing like that out on the trail.

Clay had also gotten Bill to agree to stop by his ranch so he leave the black stallion with his friend and neighbor, Marion Sooner.

Clay didn't like thinking the judge would do anything but dismiss the case once he heard the whole story, but it paid to be cautious, and he was a cautious man. Curly Beeler and his gang had run roughshod far and wide for several years, and while it couldn't be proved because Curly didn't leave witnesses, a string of deaths followed him, including a couple of Texas Rangers. Even Bill McDaniel agreed that bringing down Curly Beeler and his gang had been high on their priority list.

Ordinarily, Bill McDaniel would never have considered a side trip to the Sooner's, but during the past few days he'd come to believe Clay wasn't the murderer the judge had described him to be. This was just a man who grieved over the death of his wife at the hands of Curly and his followers. He was just a man who sought vengeance for the death of his wife and unborn child. Hell, what man wouldn't have done the same thing? He'd never felt he'd ever brought in the wrong man, until now, and that worried him to distraction. Could there have been others? He would speak to the judge about Clay.

At the Sooner's ranch, they were welcomed with open arms. Rebecca Sooner made a supper fit for a king and Marion assured Clay his place was being well taken care of. Over coffee, Bill McDaniel once more heard the story of Curly and his gang raiding Clay's ranch and the death of Clay's wife, Martha, along with them offering to come to Austin and speak to the judge on Clay's behalf.

This had been the icing on the cake, so to speak. Bill was now convinced Clay Brentwood was, in his opinion, justified to do what he'd done, the law be dammed. He'd only done what any lawman would have done had he had the opportunity, or the guts.

Curly Beeler and his gang had been the target of the rangers when two of them, sent to bring him in, up and disappeared – never to be heard from again. But without evidence, the Beeler gang once again got off free. Made a man wonder about the justice system.

The following day, Marion Sooner drove Clay and Bill McDaniel to the train station where they boarded the south bound train that would take them to Austin. The ranger's horse was in a freight car, along with several other horses, and they joked about cowboys getting lazy. Train travel was making them soft.

That evening, over supper in the dining car, the ranger stared across the table at his, so called, prisoner. During the entire trip, Clay had not seen a pair of handcuffs. “Got a question, Clay,” the ranger said after swallowing his food. “You’ve had several opportunities to escape, not being handcuffed and all; but you didn’t try even once. Why not?”

Without looking up, Clay said, “I gave my word. Besides, I didn’t kill anybody in Kansas and I feel once the judge knows the truth about Curly, he’ll up and drop all the charges. But if I ran away, that would make me look guilty, plus you’d look bad to the other rangers for not puttin’ me in irons. Don’t reckon you’d ever hear the end of it.”

The rest of the trip was almost boring; except for the talks they had about hunting down wild horses and breaking them. Bill had always wanted to do that and found it exciting to hear about. There was something about Clay that made you forget he was a wanted man, and for the first time in his long career as a Texas Ranger, he considered letting a man escape. The problem was, Clay wouldn’t go - him and his damn sense of justice could sure put a knot in a ranger’s plan.

McDaniel wired ahead that he was bringing Clay in, and when they arrived at the train station in Austin, six armed guards were waiting on them – sent by the judge.

Bill McDaniel tried to tell them they weren't needed, but the judge had given them orders and they weren't about to be swayed from their sworn duty.

People turned their heads to gawk as Bill McDaniel and Clay Brentwood walked side by side, talking amiably, while surrounded by guards with rifles: two in front, two in back and one on each side, making Clay feel a mite conspicuous.

Surrounded by armed guards, it was just now dawning on him that things might not go as easily as he had thought they would. If this judge had his mind made up, he would definitely need an attorney.

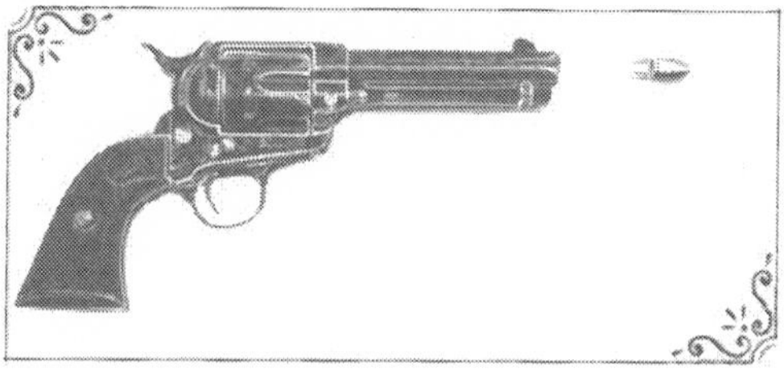

# CHAPTER FIVE

-

That night, Clay Brentwood sat on his bunk, locked behind iron bars, wondering if he had made the right decision. Shooting it out with a Texas Ranger, win, lose or draw, hadn't been an option any more than running was. Coming in voluntarily had to amount to something. The judge had to understand how things were.

But what if he couldn't convince the judge to overrule the warrants and turn him loose? What if the judge didn't believe his story? Or didn't care? After all, it would just be his word for it. It was too late to ask the people of Bristol Springs to come and testify in his behalf, or the senora, for that matter. Besides, he'd already convinced the senora that he wouldn't need any help.

And then, there was Marion Sooner and his wife, Rebecca. But what actually had they seen – nothing but the aftermath, and then it had only been Marion, and he had not actually seen Curly or his men. He only had Clay's word for it that Curly and his men did it.

Sleep was a mixture of nightmares. In one, he was standing on the gallows with a noose around his neck, looking out at a large crowd of people waiting to see him get his neck stretched. Another had him racing across the plains on the black stallion - men with guns were chasing him, bullets whizzing past his head – then the black stallion stumbled, and him going over the horse's head.

A little before daylight, Clay woke up drenched in sweat. His head ached and his hands trembled. It had only been a dream, but it had felt so real. He swung his legs over the side of the bunk and then sat up. The only noise was a slight snoring sound coming from the guard, sitting in a chair, at the far end of the hallway.

Two hours later, the jailer brought his breakfast, but the only thing Clay wanted at the moment was coffee. His stomach was too upset for food, but somehow, he forced himself to eat the bowl of mush, with no sugar or milk, hoping it would help – which, he guessed it did, or maybe it was the lukewarm coffee that tasted like yesterdays.

After breakfast, Clay sat on his bunk and smoked a cigarillo, wondering when and how he could contact a lawyer. He didn't know anybody in Austin. Maybe the jailer would know of one, but when he asked, the jailer just laughed. "I guess you don't know the honorable Horatio B. Tyson, do you, boy? Ah lawyer ain't gonna do you no good, not with this judge," he said as he carried the tin cup and bowl away, still laughing.

Clay sat back down on his bunk, elbows on his knees and his head in his hands. He was now convinced he would need the best lawyer in town, of that he was sure.

An hour later, as he paced back and forth from one end of his cell to the other, pondering his situation, the jailer opened his cell door and said, "You got ah visitor."

Following the jailer down the hall, he was puzzled. Who could it be? "Did they give ah name?" Clay asked.

The jailer shook his head, no, and stopped at a door. "In there," he said and stepped back.

Clay walked into the room and looked around. There was a table and two chairs and that was it. Seated at the table was a tall, rail thin man of about thirty, with a full head of uncontrollable red hair. His suit looked to be tailored to fit him and he was clean-shaven. When he looked up and saw Clay, he grinned, stood up and reached his hand out.

"Mister Brentwood, my name is Howard Loring. My friend, Bill McDaniel said you were in need of an attorney, and thought I might be the one who could help you."

They shook hands and then sat down across from one another.

"Bill told me what he knows about the case, but I'd like to hear your version, if you don't mind," the attorney said, taking a pen and paper from a leather satchel.

"You said Bill McDaniel, the Texas Ranger, sent you?"

"That's right. We're friends."

"Why would he do that? He's the one that arrested me and brought me here."

"Yes, funny when you think about it, isn't it? I asked him the same question and he told me after getting to know you, he believed you had just reason for what you did and wanted to help. So, he came to me, and here I am."

Clay looked long and hard at the man sitting across from him and finally decided he liked him and would trust the ranger's judgment. After all, it wasn't like he had a list to choose from.

"What's your fee?" Clay asked.

Howard Loring smiled. “A man who cuts to the chase. I like that. Yes, I like that a lot. One hundred dollars if I win.”

“And if you don’t?” Clay asked.

“I’m not in the habit of taking cases I don’t think I can win. But, I still need to hear what you have to say before I make up my mind about taking your case. If I lose, you owe me nothing. Fair enough?”

Clay nodded his head okay but didn’t like to think about the possibility of losing.

They talked for the next hour and a half. Clay told him the whole story from beginning to end. From time to time, the attorney would ask him a question, and then write notes on a sheet of paper.

When Clay finished, the attorney leaned back, filled a pipe and lit it, blowing a smoke ring in the air.

“You’re sure you don’t know this, Revers Milan?” he asked.

“I never even heard the name until the ranger brought it up,” Clay said matter of factly.

“Hum, something that’ll need some checking into - that is, if you want me for your attorney?”

Clay thought for a moment, then reached his hand across the table. "I reckon you'll do ta ride the river with. Any idea when I go in front of the judge?"

"He hasn't set a date yet, but I'll try to prod that along when I file a paper to have the whole thing dismissed. But, to be honest with you, I don't know this judge. He was appointed by someone in Washington and has only been on the bench here for less than a year, and I've not had a case in his court. Although, I have heard rumors and I... well... let me put it this way. We may have our work cut out for us."

They stood up and looked at each other. "If you come up with anything new, any little thing, tell the guard to contact me, and in the meantime, try not to worry."

The jailer opened the door and as Clay left the room, he looked over his shoulder and said, "If you were in my boots, would you worry?"

Howard Loring just stood there, staring at his client, not sure how to answer the question, so he said nothing.

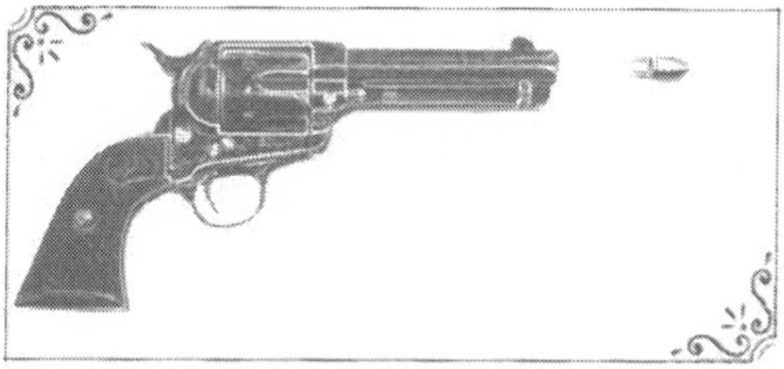

# CHAPTER SIX

Lightning filled the sky, causing ghostlike shadows to dance on the walls of Clay's cell as he sat on his bunk and reviewed everything his attorney had told him.

Curly's sister had filed the charge of murder against him, telling the judge that her brother, Charles, was an honest businessman who bought and sold cattle. He'd told her that he thought someone he'd bested in a deal had started the rumor that he was a thief, which was a lie. She didn't know why this, this, Clay Brentwood murdered her dearly departed brother, but witnesses saw him do it in cold blood, and she wanted him punished for it.

Apparently, the judge believed her and had issued the warrant for his arrest. As for the warrant for the murder of Revers Milan, that came about because the judge had accidentally knocked a pile of wanted posters from his desk onto the floor, and when he went to pick them up, he noticed one with Clay's name on it and added it to the one he issued for Curly. He felt it would be easier to convict a man for two felonies than for one.

Clay racked his brain until it hurt, trying to figure out who this Revers Milan was, but came up with nothing. How could he be accused of murdering someone he'd never met or had any knowledge of? It just didn't make any sense.

Exhausted, he fell into a deep and troublesome sleep.

The following morning when the jailer told him his mouthpiece wanted to see him, Clay hurried down the hall and entered the room. After the amenities were taken care of, Clay asked him what he'd found out.

"I went to see Mister Beeler's sister. Her name is Abigail Schuster. She's been a widow for the past ten years and is a dyed in the wool, bible thumping, Sunday school teacher, who goes to the same church as the judge. She's a fetching woman and word has it, our judge has been seen on several occasions, coming from her house late at night. I tried to talk to her, but she told me the judge told her not to speak to anyone about the case, then slammed the door in my face."

Clay sat there, not knowing what to say. The woman had to realize her brother was a liar. There were wanted posters for him posted everywhere. Surely, she had seen them. Things like this just didn't happen, did they? Was the justice system so corrupt that a woman could use her wily ways to get a judge to do what she wanted?

"Now, about this, Revers Milan," the attorney said, bringing Clay back from his thoughts. "After contacting a friend of mine up in Wichita, he did some snooping around, and telegraphed me back just a little while ago. His telegram said Milan was shot in the back of the head, on a clear moonlit night, just as he was walking up to the front door of his home, about one o'clock in the morning. His wife had opened the door and got a good look at the man who did it. Apparently, the man was no more than ten feet away. Without a word, he turned and walked away. The description she gave to the sheriff fit you to a tee. Another source told my friend that somewhere around midnight that same night, a man by the name of, Simon Snodgrass, said he saw you standing in front of the saloon, arguing with this Milan fella over a poker game. My friend said the whole thing took place about five years ago. Wasn't that around the time you moved from Kansas to Texas, and bought a ranch?"

Clay shook his head. "This is crazy. I have no idea who this Revers Milan is, and I didn't kill him. And to answer your question - yes, that's about the time I bought my ranch down in Texas. I had just gotten married and I had money I'd made from roundin' up wild horses and breakin'em. I sold'em to ranchers around the area. That's where I got the money to put down on the ranch in Texas. I bought the place from a widow woman whose husband had fallen from a horse and broke his neck. And just for the record, I've never sat in on a poker game in my life. I work too hard for my money ta have some card shark cheat me out of it. This Snodgrass fella, who I don't know either, is mistaken. Has to been somebody who looks like me, cause it wasn't me."

"Well, we'll know soon enough," the attorney, said, writing something on a piece of paper he had lying on the table.

"What are you talkin' about?" Clay asked.

He looked up from his writing to get a look at Clay's face when he delivered this next piece of information. "Wanting to set the record straight, I took the liberty of sending train tickets to both, the widow, Mrs. Milan and the other man, Simon Snodgrass. They're both coming in on the train day after tomorrow, and I'm hoping they can clear up the charges against you for Milan's death."

"Good," Clay said with a determined look on his face. "That should settle that matter once and for all. Now, let's talk some more about Curly's sister. Any chance we can talk some sense into her head?"

Howard was glad Clay didn't seem worried about Mrs. Milan or Simon Snodgrass showing up. That made believing the man, easier. "I honestly don't know," he said, "I tried talking the judge into letting her to talk to me, and he told me flat, to stay away from her. The only good news is, the judge won't set a date for your hearing until after the people from Wichita have arrived, which gives me a little more time to prepare my case. The bad news is, the judge has decided he will try the case his self, which means there will be no jury. I tried to argue with him but got nowhere. He's a strange duck if ever I saw one. But even so, we should be all right, especially if the people from Wichita say you're not the one they saw," Howard said, tilting his head to one side and smiling.

They shook hands and Clay was taken back to his cell. When he got there, he saw a mountain of dirty rags sitting on his bunk, which turned out to be a giant of a man wrapped up in a filthy buffalo robe. The man was as dirty as his clothes were, and he stunk something awful. Turning his head, Clay looked over his shoulder at the guard, who just grinned and raised his hands, palms forward.

Anger began to rise inside him. He was tired of being a nice guy. "That's my bunk you're sittin' on," Clay said matter of factly.

The man looked up and grinned, showing a mouth full of brown, tobacco stained teeth. "That so? Well, it's mine, now."

"You need ta get off my bunk, mister, and I mean, get off of it, now!"

"And if I don't, what're you gonna do about it?"

Without another word, Clag grabbed the man's shaggy hair with both hands and jerked him forward, then slammed the man's face against his knee, anger taking control of his actions. The man let out a groan and grabbed Clay around the waist and picked him off the floor. Driving his shoulder into Clay's stomach, he slammed Clay against the far wall, which didn't hurt Clay as bad as the man hoped. Clay had worked hard all his life, wrestling steers and breaking wild horses and he was well muscled. But he had to admit, this man could and would hurt him bad, if he didn't do something quick. It was like fighting a wild animal.

Out of the corner of his right eye, he saw three guards standing outside the cell, watching. They had grins on their faces and money in their fists. This was a setup and he was the rube. He didn't figure any of them were betting on him, just betting on how long it would take the big man to put him face down on the cell floor.

Shoving the man back, Clay stepped to the side and drove a right to the side of the man's head, then stepped in and hit him with an uppercut to the chin.

Instead of going down like an ordinary man should have, the giant grinned and wiped blood from his mouth on the sleeve of his coat.

"I like it when they fight back, makes it more interestin', but when I get done with you sonny boy, there ain't gonna be much ta clean up and I'll collect ten dollars jest fer havin' ah bit of fun," the giant said as he rushed forward with both arms spread wide.

Clay swallowed and knew he was in trouble if he didn't do something and do it now. He figured the only thing he could do, would be to keep out of the giant's grasp. If the man got his arms around him again, he would break his back, which would finish the fight, and him.

Ducking under the man's arms, Clay drove a hard right to the big fella's kidney area and hoped for the best. The heavy clothes the man wore absorbed some of the blow, but not all of it.

The big man gave a grunt and swung around. A backhand against Clay's jaw that felt like a club, instead of a fist, sent him sprawling across the cell - his head and back slamming against the bars. Bright lights flashed behind his eyes and he fought to keep from losing consciousness. Everything was a blur, and he was seeing two of everything.

The big man grabbed him by the shirt and pulled him to his feet, pushing his face close to Clay's. "Now we'll see if you can fly," he said. The man's breath was enough to make him pass out and it was almost a relief to be lifted like a sack of potatoes and thrown toward the back wall.

Clay landed against the back wall of the cell and slid down to the floor, pain now wracking every muscle in his body and the wind had been knocked out of him. He knew he had to do something, but what? He couldn't take much more of this. Getting to his feet, he held out his hands, motioning for more. "Is that all you got? I thought ah big tub of guts like you could hit better than that. I knew ah girl once who could hit harder than you."

Clay got exactly the response he wanted as the big man charged, yelling at the top of his voice, “You’re gonna wish you hadn’t said that!”

Clay slipped under the charge and stuck his foot out, catching the man on the shins, which threw him off balance and he went headlong into the wall and bounced back, somewhat dazed. Wasting no time, Clay stepped up behind him and kicked him squarely between the legs.

Suddenly, the big man’s voice sounded like an opera singer as he grabbed his crotch with both hands. Clay jumped into the air and kicked the man in the back with both feet, driving his head against the wall a second time. Then, before he could recover, Clay drove hard punches into the man’s kidney and liver area. Next, he hit the man as hard as he could on the left ear. He heard the man’s eardrum pop and watched as blood began to seep from the ear.

Stepping in close, he was about to deliver the final blows that would put the big man face down on the floor, when he heard the cell door open and the last thing he remembered was three guards beating on him with clubs.

Clay came to consciousness slowly. He opened his eyes and looked around. He was no longer in his cell. The room was six feet by six feet and had no windows. The walls and door were solid. There was no bed or chair. Except for him, and a wooden bucket sitting in the corner, the room was empty. "So, this is what solitary looks like," he said to himself.

Taking survey, he counted several knots on his head that ached like blue-blazes. His ribs were badly bruised, which made it hard to breathe. He had a broken nose that also made it hard to breathe. Looking down, he saw that his nose had bled on the front of his shirt. The left side of his face was black and blue, and both eyes were swollen almost closed. Other than that, he was alive, which was better than the alternative they had in store for him.

Then he wondered if they really wanted him dead, or did they just want him badly beaten, looking like he'd gone ten rounds with a grizzly bear? If they had wanted him dead, surely the guards could have done it, and blamed it on the giant.

A hinged piece at the bottom of the door swung up and a bowl of mush and a cup of water came sliding in. When the piece swung back down, Clay heard the loud click of a bolt being driven home, securing the swinging door in place, then nothing.

In the semi-dark cell, Clay used his fingers to scoop up the mush and then he drank the water. It had been a long day and he lay down on the floor and slept. Right now, rest was what he needed. He was too exhausted to even dream.

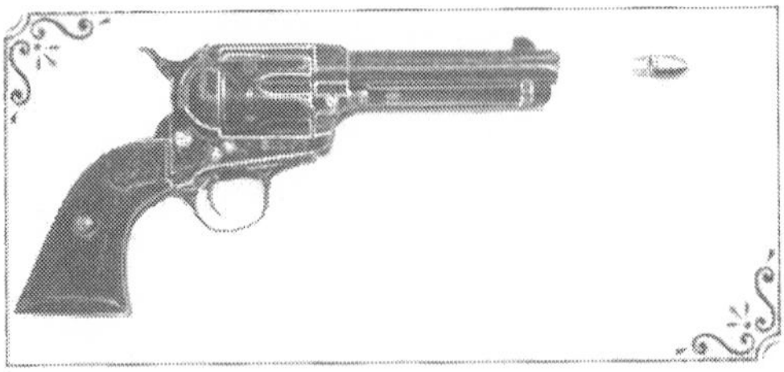

# CHAPTER SEVEN

Three days later, Clay had just finished eating his morning bowl of mush when a guard opened the door allowing light to come flooding into the room, nearly blinding him. “Let’s go, tough guy,” the guard said. “The judge wants you up in the courtroom.”

“Do I get a chance to clean up some before I go see him?” Clay asked.

“No time. The judge wants to see you now, and he ain’t much on waitin’.”

Even though he knew the courtroom was open to the public, Clay was surprised to see so many people. The room was almost full. It seemed word about a man facing two murder charges had gotten around fast and there were those who needed some entertainment.

When he was escorted into the room, there was a loud gasp, and then the room got quiet as a tomb. Their mouths were hanging open as they stared at a severely beaten man in filthy, blood-covered clothes. Out of the quiet, the courtroom was suddenly ablaze with whispers that sounded like a hive of bees.

The look on Howard Loring's face said volumes. He was astonished by the way Clay looked and rushed over and helped him to his seat. "What happened to you?" he whispered. "They told me you'd started a fight with one of the other prisoners, but…"

Clay looked at Howard. "I didn't start the fight. Somebody wanted ta pretty me up some before I come ta meet the judge."

Clay felt a hand on his shoulder and looked back. The hand belonged to the head of the rangers, Bill McDaniel, and sitting on the bench on the right side of him was his old neighbors, Marion and Rebecca Sooner. Next to them was Ned Baker, owner of the mercantile in Bristol Springs. On the ranger's left sat, looking like she'd just stepped out of a picture book, was the beautiful, Senora Ontiveros. Tears were streaming down her face as she stared at him. All, but the senora, began talking at once – wanting to know what had happened? Marion Sooner said, "This is an outrage! How can the court system allow this to happen?"

"You've got friends," Howard Loring said. "They just started arriving, saying they were here on your behalf."

Clay was stunned to see them and for a brief moment he felt a wave of emotion pass over him. Clay, not wanting to show any weakness, clenched his teeth until it passed. Even so, he was touched.

The judge slammed his gavel down, hard, several times, staring at Clay's friends. "Order in the court! Order in the court!" he said in a high squeaky voice. "You will be respectful and quiet in my court or I'll have all of you escorted out, and you'll not come back, no matter why you're here! Is that understood?"

The courtroom quieted down and Clay's friends sat back, nodding their heads. After coming all this way to help him, none of them wanted to be thrown out of the courtroom before they had their say.

Judge Tyson leaned back in his high-backed chair and stared at the prisoner. 'My gawd, that must have been some fight,' he thought to himself. 'Wish I could have seen it.'

One of the guards said this man, Clay Brentwood, was in the process of whipping Bear Griswald when they had to step in and pull him off of Griswald before he was killed. That he knew of, no one had ever whipped the Bear, which just went to show what kind of man this Brentwood was – a deadly, bloodthirsty killer just as Abigail had said.

Coming out of his thoughts, he noticed Bill McDaniel sitting behind the prisoner. Judge Tyson leaned forward and asked, "Mister McDaniel, does the head of the Texas Rangers have some purpose for sitting with the prisoner?"

Bill McDaniel stood up. "Yes sir, I do. After spending time with the prisoner, Clay Brentwood, it is my considered opinion, he has been falsely charged and I recommend all charges against him be dropped."

The judge nodded his head and said, "Is that so? And may I ask if your opinion was solicited by the court?"

"No sir, I came here on my own accord," Bill McDaniel said.

"I see," the judge said with a slight grin on his thin lips. "Well then, since your opinion was not asked for, it will not be allowed in my court. You are excused."

As Bill McDaniel turned and headed for the door, Howard Loring jumped to his feet. "Your honor, this man is on my list of character witnesses."

"Then I suggest you remove him. This is my courtroom and I make the rules, and as the arresting officer, he will not be allowed to testify on behalf of the accused. Now, sit down before I cite you for contempt."

Howard Loring sat down, slowly, and wrote something on a piece of paper, then handed it to a man sitting behind him on the seat next to the aisle. The man scanned the note, then rose and left the courtroom.

The judge watched the transaction and wondered what that was all about - but in the end it made no difference. This was his courtroom and these backwater hicks could do nothing to him, he was the judge and his word was law.

By noon, the judge was seething with anger. The first two people who had been called to the witness stand, Silvia Milan, wife of the murdered, Revers Milan, and Simon Snodgrass, the man who'd witnessed the argument in front of the saloon, both from Wichita, had stated under oath that the defendant was not the man they'd seen. They admitted that he looked somewhat like the man they saw, and when the judge asked them if they might be mistaken, it being dark and all, they stated they were sure - this was not the man they'd seen.

In the end, he'd had to withdraw the charge and this did not make him happy. He had envisioned sentencing Clay Brentwood for multiple murder charges in various parts of the country. That would have shown Bill McDaniel and that upstart lawyer of his, Howard Loring, what kind of man they were siding.

Exasperated by the way things were going; he called a one-hour lunch break to prepare for the Beeler case. He didn't want to lose this one.

As he entered his office, Abigail Schuster ran over to him and threw her arms around his neck. "Oh Horatio, I am so sorry. Those people must have been paid off. I understand Mister Brentwood is well to do. What are we going to do, now?"

The judge removed her arms and she stepped back, embarrassed. "I'm sorry, I didn't mean to be so forward," she said, brushing her dress, then checking her hair.

"What are you doing here?" Horatio asked. "We shouldn't be seen together until the trial is over."

"Yes, of course, dear. I will leave."

As she started for the side door, the judge called her back. "Abigail, are you sure everything you told me about your brother is true?" He had seen the wanted posters.

"Oh yes! My brother was nothing more than someone who bought and sold cattle and horses. He was God fearing; a church going man, who was wrongly accused by men he'd bested in trading deals, and that beast who calls himself a man, sitting out there, looking so smug, murdered my poor brother in cold blood! If ever a man needed punished for what he did, it's him. Promise me you'll see justice done!"

The judge escorted her to the side door and said, "Don't you worry your pretty little head about it. You just let me handle things. I'll see you in the courtroom in about an hour."

When she'd gone, the judge rushed over to his desk and opened one of his law books to where a marker was sticking out, and after a moment, closed it, smiling. He had the man right where he wanted him and there was no way for him to wiggle out of it.

Victory would taste good.

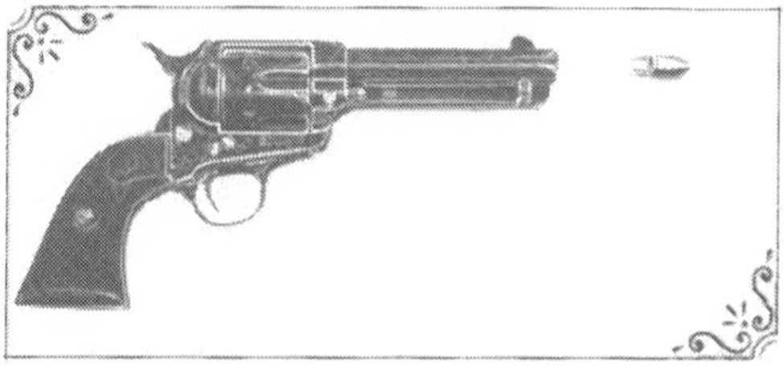

# CHAPTER EIGHT

During the one-hour lunch break, Clay sat in his cell eating the best meal he'd had since being thrown into this pigsty. Senora Ontiveros had it delivered, along with a doctor to see to his wounds and clean clothes for him to wear.

The guards had protested, but when Bill McDaniel, head of the Texas Rangers, threw his weight around, they backed down.

It was a completely different Clay Brentwood who walked into the courtroom for the afternoon session, walking erect and proud, and surer of himself than he had been earlier. Both he and his lawyer felt better since the warrant for the murder of Revers Milan had been dropped. It gave them hope.

When the judge walked in and took his seat, he was astonished at the change in not only the look of the defendant, but his attitude as well. He glared at the guard, who shrugged his shoulders, mouthing, "It was Senora Ontiveros and Captain McDaniel."

The afternoon went pretty much as the judge figured it might. Surprisingly, this young upstart, Howard Loring, was a superb attorney who brought in a very convincing group of people to testify on the prisoner's behalf. When the senora took the stand, every male in the room sat up a bit straighter and the women eyed her with envy. She was not only very beautiful, but also, educated and wealthy.

Judge Tyson noticed how she looked at the accused, sitting there so confident and handsome in his suit, and he envied him. Why did so many people think of this man as a hero? He was a murderer of innocent men. Did they all believe the lies posted about Mister Beeler?

His neighbors from here in Texas, the Sooners - how detailed their testimonies had been, and what a looker Rebecca Sooner was, sitting there on the witness stand, looking so pretty and innocent, then coming to tears when talking about this man's wife. Obviously, since they had not actually seen the killing, and knew only what Clay Brentwood had told them, their testimony as far as he was concerned, meant nothing. It was only based on hearsay. Mister Brentwood, he was convinced, conjured up the whole thing and would say anything to save his hide.

Even the mercantile owner, what was his name, oh yes, Ned Baker, from down in New Mexico where the accused had murdered Mister Beeler in cold blood; he too had presented a glowing testimony that, unbeknownst to them, had given him the answer he was looking for; the one fact that everyone except him, seemed to have overlooked. But the clincher had been the accused, himself. Under oath, he admitted he had, with premeditated murder in mind, stalked Charles "Curly" Beeler and his associates and then gunned them down without mercy. And, not only had he shot Mister Beeler, he had taken a knife and cut his throat, causing Mister Beeler a slow and agonizing death.

At four o'clock, when the prisoner stepped down from the witness box, Judge Horatio B. Tyson looked out over the room, rapped his gavel, and declared he would render his decision at nine o'clock the following morning, and then left the people in the courtroom in utter frustration.

Before being taken back to his cell, Howard Loring assured Clay there was no way the judge could do anything but set him free. The others agreed and told him not to worry. But as the guard marched him away, the look on his face showed he wasn't as confident as they were. The judge had a look about him that he didn't like. There was nothing he could pinpoint, but it was there; his gut told him so.

That night, the judge and Abigail had a private dinner at her house where he assured her everything was under control. It was after midnight when he finally crept out her back door and took the side streets to his private quarters on the top floor of the courthouse.

Howard Loring had dinner with the man he'd given the note to. His name was John Price, a Pinkerton Detective. He and Howard had gone to school together and the man just happened to be passing through town.

"Got yourself a winner with this one, Howard. Tyson was transferred out here by a group of senators from Washington. Got himself a reputation of being a hell-fire and brimstone preacher on Sunday and a hanging judge the rest of the week. Made a lot of enemies back in the Capital, including some married women and widow ladies. Rumor has it, he is not happy being here. But he has no choice. It was come here or face disbarment proceedings."

Howard thanked his friend and suddenly didn't feel quite so confident. That night, he paced the floor and checked and rechecked his law books, finding nothing the judge could use against his client except one thing; but surely the judge wouldn't go that route; not with all the evidence, and what Clay had gone through.

The following morning, every seat was taken and people were standing against the back wall, wondering what the judge was up to? Surely, the judge had to dismiss the case. The man was only avenging the death of his wife and unborn child, as any man would do. Even the head of the Texas Rangers had wanted to stand up for him.

Clay was brought into the courtroom looking tired, like he hadn't slept all night, which he hadn't. That nagging feeling wouldn't go away and he'd paced his cell.

Once he was seated, the judge banged his gavel and looked down at Clay. "Mister Brentwood would you mind taking the stand again. I have something I need to clear up before I make my decision.

"But your honor…" Howard Loring protested.

"Just something I need to clarify," the judge said, waving his hand as though it was really nothing at all.

As Clay approached the witness chair, the hair on the back of his neck stood up. There was something about the look in the judge's eyes and that nagging feeling came back.

When Clay was sworn in and seated, the judge looked down at him and said in a gentle voice, "Mister Brentwood, yesterday you testified that you followed Mister Beeler all the way from Texas to the New Mexico Territory. Is that true?"

Clay looked at the judge with a questioning look. "Yes sir. Took two and a half years."

"And during all that time, you never had thoughts that you might be chasing the wrong man?"

"No sir," Clay said in as confident of a voice as he could muster.

"And when you finally caught up to him and his associates, in the town of Bristol Springs, you rode into town with the intent of serving as judge and jury over their fate. Is that correct?"

"I object!" Howard Loring shouted.

"To what?" the judge asked. "I asked the accused a simple question, requiring only a simple answer. Objection overruled. Now sit down."

Turning back to Clay, he said," Please answer the question, Mister Brentwood. A yes or no will suffice."

Clay swallowed and looked down at his feet, his mind going back to that day and admitting to himself, that is exactly what he'd done.

He looked up at the judge and said, "Yes, I guess I did, but with good reason. He murdered my wife and unborn child! Your honor, the good book says, an eye for an eye. Curly Beeler and his gang were evil men. And there was no sheriff to go to, Curly had already killed him and treed the town."

The room erupted with loud whispering.

The judge waited for the room to calm down and then he looked down and said, "sheriff or no sheriff, Mister Brentwood, there is never a reason for a person to take the law into his or her own hands."

He waited a moment to let that soak in before he said, "You are excused, Mister Brentwood. Please go back to your seat."

Howard Loring stood up and said, "Your Honor, if the court will allow, I would like to ask my client a question or two, to clear up certain details."

"Denied. The court has all the information it needs to rule on this case. Please, Mister Loring, if you and your client will face me, I am ready to render my decision."

When Clay turned around and faced the judge, his attorney and all of his friends, including Bill McDaniel, stood with him.

The judge shook his head and said, under his breath, "So be it."

After a long pause, the judge said, "I decided to oversee this case myself because a letter of the law is at issue here that I feel might be overlooked by a jury. Jurors have a tendency to be swayed by sentiment, which of course as a judge, I am not allowed that privilege. I must listen to both sides of the case and abide by the letter of the law, only." The judge looked out over the room full of people and let his words sink in.

When he was satisfied, he said, "First, we heard from Miss Abigail Schuster, sister, and only relative of the deceased, Charles Beeler. Under oath, she told us of the man she knew her brother to be. She testified that he was a God-fearing man who had never harmed another living soul. She testified that he bought and sold horses and cattle for a living – nothing more. A church going woman of high regard, who only wants justice for her brother's untimely death, gave this evidence to us after swearing on a bible.

"Whereas, the accused gives us a completely different story as to Mister Beeler's character; one that shows him as a criminal who went around stealing and killing like a man with no conscious whatsoever. Remember this, Mister Beeler's character is not on trial here, so it matters not, which side of the law he was on. Mister Brentwood also admitted in this courtroom, to following Mister Beeler and his associates from Texas to the New Mexico Territory over a period of more than two years, with one purpose, and one purpose only, in mind. That purpose was to act as the judge, jury and executioner of Charles Beeler and his associates."

The judge took another short pause to allow this information to sink in. He didn't want anyone to say he had not explained his actions.

After catching up to Charles "Curly" Beeler and his associates, with premeditated action, which he admitted to here in this courtroom, he murdered them in cold blood."

Taking another pause, the judge took a drink of water laced with a smidgen of gin, from the glass standing next to his gavel, and then looked down at Clay. "Mister Brentwood, to the law, it makes no difference whether the man was what you claimed him to be, or not - one cannot take the law into their own hands, no matter what you feel your justification is. Otherwise, there would be no need for courts, judges, or juries. Our system of law, as we know it, would not be worth the paper it is written on."

He took another sip of water, taking his time, savoring his victory - letting them stand there in silence, suffering from his final words.

"Once again, I must remind you, the letter of the law is at stake in this case, not sentiment. Therefore, Mister Brentwood, it is the ruling of this court that you are found guilty of premeditated murder in the first degree. It is further decreed that you shall be transported to the prison at Huntsville, where, at a date yet to be determined, you will be hung by the neck until you are dead."

He stood up and banged his gavel. "This case is closed. Court is adjourned." And before anyone recovered from their shock, he vanished into his chamber.

The judge had just taken his robe off and was hanging it on the coat rack next to the door when Abigail came charging into his office and threw herself into his arms. "Oh, Horatio, you were magnificent!" she said, kissing his face.

Horatio pushed her gently away and smiled at her - dinner this evening?

She nodded her head, yes. "Whatever you want, my dear, whatever your heart desires."

When she'd gone, he lit a cigar and poured himself a small glass of gin from the bottle hidden in his desk drawer. One needed to be allowed a few small pleasures in life, he thought to himself as he took a drink of gin – like doing favors for women, especially, widow women. There were so many rewards.

Whatever was said to Clay as the guard took him back to his cell, he heard none of it, his mind was far away. He was walking in a fog. They were going to hang him for avenging his wife's murder. His life was over just like that and there wasn't a damn thing he could do about it, or was there? There had to be some way out of this mess. Could he appeal to a higher court? He was sure his attorney had done everything he could to get the case dropped. And what about all the people who had come so far, at their own expense, to testify on his behalf? It was like the judge had ignored them. It was that woman, that Abigail, who had warped his mind, probably with sexual favors.

Clay laid down on his bunk and put his hands under his head. He couldn't let this feeling of despair get the best of him. There had to be a way out of this mess. He just had to figure out what it was.

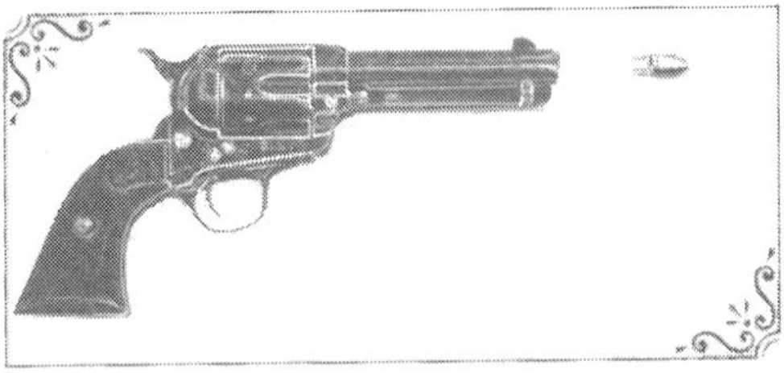

# CHAPTER NINE

An hour later, Clay was taken to the visitor's room to meet with Howard Loring, who apologized over and over, saying he would find a way to see the governor. He vowed to somehow make him see the wrong the judge had done and get the verdict overturned.

Clay didn't hold much hope, since the governor had refused to see Howard, earlier.

Back in his cell, the clanging of the cell door closing and the turning of the key would have sealed most men's fates for them, but not Clay Brentwood.

He walked over and looked out of the window, trying to clear the fog from his mind. He needed to think straight. The late afternoon sun was creeping toward the western horizon, sending its rays through the lazy puffs of white clouds that drifted across the sky, making them glow a light pink.

"Better take a long look, mister, cause when the hangman slips that black hood over yer head, you won't be seein' nuthin' after that," the guard said as he walked away, twirling the ring of keys on his finger.

Had anyone ever escaped from Huntsville prison? He didn't know. But with the prison being fairly new and him being in the New Mexico Territory these past several years, how could he know. How many men had they hung there, he wondered?

He'd just walked over and sat down on his bunk when the guard returned. "You got visitors, so shake ah leg, I ain't got all day," he said, unlocking the door.

Once again, he followed the guard down the hallway toward the visiting room. What if I over powered him right now and escaped? How far would I get, he wondered? Something in the back of his mind said, this wasn't the right time, so he waited.

The visitor's room was filled with, Howard, the senora, Ned Baker and the Sooners. They were standing in front of the table and all began talking at the same time.

"Are you all right?" "How are they treating you?" "Don't worry, we're going to see the governor."

Clay held up his hands, wondering how his attorney had sneaked them in? The judge had said his attorney was the only one to visit him. Maybe, since the trial was over, it didn't make any difference, now. "Whoa, one at a time," he said, grinning from ear to ear.

When they'd quieted down, his attorney said, "Like I said earlier, I'm going to the governor to see if I can get the judge's decision overturned."

Marion Sooner stepped over and shook his hand. "Everything is gonna work out, Clay, you'll see. And your place will be waitin' on you when you come home."

The senora was standing to the side and when Clay looked over at her, she said, "I will be working closely with Senor' Loring and we will see you freed."

Clay attempted a grin, but it fell short. "I appreciate all of you tryin' ta help and all, but that judge is pretty smart and the truth is, I knew I was breakin' the law when I rode in there, that day. I stopped by the sheriff's office, but Curly had already killed him. At that point I felt I had no choice but to see them in hell where they belonged."

"And you did right," Ned Baker said. "You saved the whole town by doing what you did, and I'll, by gawd, tell the governor so."

Back in his cell, Clay finally smiled and the guard didn't like it. "What you got ta smile about, Brentwood? They're gonna hang you by the neck until yer daid. You ever seen ah man hung? They wiggle and squirm and jump around and most of 'em mess their pants. It ain't no way ta die. And, I understand your life at Huntsville while yer ah waitin', ain't gonna be no picnic, either. It's ah hell hole if ever there was one."

Clay watched the guard walk away, laughing. He was at least thirty pounds overweight for his height, which was about five foot ten inches. He was sloppy about his appearance and he had a mean streak in him. Clay wondered if that was part of what it took to become a jail guard, mean and stupid. Being this was the first time he'd ever been in jail, he didn't know.

For the next several days, right after breakfast, he was shackled and taken down to the livery stable where he worked all day, under guard. He did all the dirty work the liveryman didn't want to do, like cleaning the stalls and hauling bales of hay down from the loft and scattering them around the inside the stalls - cleaning harness and general work around the place. And when he needed to use a tool, such as a pitchfork, two guards with rifles pointed at him, would stand far enough away so he wouldn't have a chance to attack them and possibly escape.

On the seventh day after being sentenced, Howard Lorning watched Clay enter the visitor's room and was shocked. He was not only filthy, but he also stunk. He hadn't been allowed to shave and had a heavy growth of beard. He looked like one of those deep woods characters described in the dime novels.

Without a word, he left the room and went straight to the head jailer's office and demanded they allow Clay to clean up.

"What for?" the jailer asked. "They'll be taking him to Huntsville before long and he will be their problem then."

"Have you no decency?" Howard asked, shocked at the jailer's attitude.

The jailer shrugged his shoulders and made a 'harrumph sound.' "I don't see where it makes any difference whether he's filthy or all gussied up. He'll dance at the end of a rope, whether he's dirty or clean, just like anybody else."

Howard stormed out of the jailer's office and headed straight for the ranger's office, which was just down the street.

Bill McDaniel was doing what he hated more than anything - paperwork, so when the bell over the door clanged, he was glad to get a reprieve.

When Howard told him the story and solicited his help, Bill pulled out a pipe and filled the bowl, then put fire to the tobacco, drawing several times to get it going good. Chewing tobacco was for when he was out in the open where he could spit.

"I'd like to help you, Howard, I really would; but the judge told me in no uncertain terms, to stay away from having any dealings with you, Clay, or those other folks who want to help him. I'm sorry, but he'd have my badge and I'm not quite ready to give it up."

Howard nodded his head, understanding the rangers' position. He was about to ask the ranger another question when he remembered leaving Clay standing in the visitor's room. He turned and headed for the door, speaking over his shoulder "It's alright Bill, I understand. I kind of figured as much. I'll work something out."

"Hold on Howard," the ranger said. "There just might be another way, one where I wouldn't have to get involved. Do you have any money?"

Two hours later, Clay walked into the visitor's room to once again meet with his attorney, forgiving him for running off like he'd done.

Howard looked at him and grinned. Clay looked like his old self, bathed, fresh shaved and wearing clean clothes the Senora had sent.

"How'd you get them to let me clean up, you bribe somebody?" Clay asked with a grin a mile wide.

"As a matter of fact, that's exactly what I did. It was the ranger's idea to use bribery, and when he broached the subject, I remembered you'd given me some money to hold for you right before we got here, and as it turns out, jailers don't make much of a salary. I'll tell you, Clay, that twenty-dollar gold piece made his eyes light up, like you wouldn't believe."

"Well, all I can say is, thanks. It feels good to be clean, again."

"It was the senora who furnished the clean clothes and also saw to it that you will get decent meals brought in to you every evening as long as you're here. One meal a day was the best we could do, but we figured that was better than none. The lady from the restaurant will be bringing your supper to you around six each evening."

Clay sat down in the only other chair and Howard shoved a small box across the table toward him. "Thought you might like these."

The label read, Duke of Durham. "Are these tailor-made cigarettes?"

Howard shook his head, yes. "Owner of the mercantile store just started selling them. Has them shipped in from North Carolina. Fella by the name of James Bonsack got the idea of packaging them and now I understand he's getting rich."

"Well now, I do believe I've seen everthing," Clay said. "I've heard about 'em but these are the first I've ever seen. How do they taste?"

Howard pulled a box of stick matches out of his satchel and shoved them across the table. "You'll have to judge for yourself. I think you might want to keep them hidden from the guards."

After lighting up and taking a few puffs, he looked at his attorney and nodded his head in approval. "Any news?" Clay asked.

Howard shook his head from side to side. "I've been to the governor's office three times to see him and got turned down three times. One of the underlings over there told me the judge has had dinner with the governor twice since the trial, and you can bet he gave him an ear full. Probably why he won't see me."

The truth was, he was close to hitting the nail on the head. Judge Tyson had indeed filled the governor's head with lies and convinced him that Clay Brentwood was a no-good killer who deserved to be hung. He'd also advised the governor against talking to Clay's attorney, Howard Loring, who would say anything to get his client off.

The governor, just wanting to finish his term so he could go back to his home just outside of Dallas, and write his memoirs, decided to keep himself away from the whole Brentwood affair. He had no stomach for this sort of thing. Hanging was such an ugly business and Judge Tyson had assured him he had handled it to the letter of the law, so there was no need for him to get involved.

"So that's it? They're gonna ship me off to Huntsville and hang me and there's not a damn thing I can do about it? Is that what you're tellin' me?" Clay's face was red and his eyes showed anger and frustration.

Howard looked at Clay and said, "I didn't say that. No, I didn't mean that at all. I'm not ready to throw in the towel just yet. I know where he lives and if I have to, I'll go there and speak to him. If I can just get him to listen to reason… I…"

"Thanks for the smokes," Clay said as he stood up, tucking the cigarettes and matches inside his shirt. He wasn't up to listening to any more excuses. He could feel a headache coming on. It wasn't that Howard didn't try hard, but for some reason, the man found it almost impossible to get any positive results, and that's what he needed right now; something to hope for.

Howard nodded and watched him leave. He felt like he'd failed Clay and wasn't sure how he was going to make things right, but he pledged to himself that he would. Somehow, he would make the governor listen to reason even though, according to the letter of the law, the judge had been right – Clay had ridden into Bristol Springs with killing Curly and his men, his reason for being there. And he had done so; there was no arguing that. There had been a whole town full of witnesses; plus, Clay had admitted it to the judge, under oath. His only plea to the governor would be that Clay had been under the strain of losing his wife and unborn child. Plus, the fact that Curly and his men had paper on them in the connection of possibly murdering two Texas Rangers, cattle and horse rustling and killing a whole bunch of other unnamed folks, which in his mind, should account for something.

The senora was the only one of Clay's supporters still here. The others had left a couple of days after the trial was over. But, before they had gone, they gave a written statement as to what they knew, in case he might need them.

Howard would be having dinner with the senora later that very evening and she would have questions he didn't have answers for, and that frustrated him. He hoped she might have some ideas on how to get Clay released, other than busting him out, which was not really an option, since that would make him look even more guilty.

At dinner that night, the senora informed Howard that she had gotten a telegram from her foreman, Ramon, requesting she come back to take care of some important business.

"I'm sorry," she said. "I don't see there is any more I can do here, and I am needed back at my ranchero." Reaching into her pocket, she asked, "Do you need any money?"

"No," Howard said, raising his hands up, palms forward. "Mister Brentwood left me money to hold for him until he gets out. I can use that for whatever he needs."

"Please tell him I have tried several times to see him but the judge will not permit it."

"I know," Howard said. "The judge only allows me to see him because I'm his attorney and he has to."

The senora noticed the look on his face and she felt a pain like someone had stabbed her in the heart. He knew he was fighting a losing battle. She reached across the table and laid her hand on his. "Please, don't give up. You must find a way," she said, knowing in her heart, there wasn't; at least nothing she knew of.

Howard Loring looked across the table and saw tears in her eyes. "Don't worry, I will find a way, somehow," he said, not sure he believed his own words.

Howard watched her walk out the door, and, at that moment, he felt… he didn't know exactly what he felt, but whatever it was, it wasn't good. A good man might die in a few days because he had not done his job properly.

As he left the restaurant, thunder rolled across the sky and large drops of rain began to fall; the first in some time and would be welcomed by most of the folks in and around Austin, but Howard didn't seem to notice as he walked toward the small house he lived in. It was only a few blocks away. He'd rented it from a widow lady who'd moved back to Arkansas after her husband had died. It was cheap rent, but it was clean and he had a roof over his head. He would spend the night, once again, searching his law books for something, anything that would help his client. He didn't have much hope, but he would search, anyway.

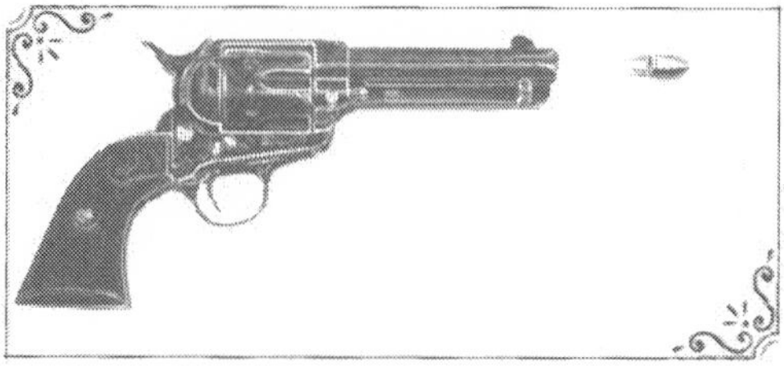

# CHAPTER TEN

That same evening, Clay was standing next to the window of his cell, staring out at the rain and people hurrying past when he saw a carriage come down the street, headed for the train station. Sitting inside was the senora. She looked out of the window and saw him. They stared at each other for only a moment, and then she waved, mouthing the words, “I’m sorry. I have to go back.”

Clay nodded and placed his palm against the bars to let her know he understood, and then placed two fingers of his left hand to his forehead. He continued watching until she was out of sight, and then looked up at the pale moon. He hadn’t understood what she’d tried to say and wondered why she was leaving? Maybe there was trouble back at the ranchero, which was likely. Or, maybe she’d just plumb given up. He couldn’t blame her if she had. Even his attorney seemed to be fighting a losing the battle. The judge had beaten him on every point.

For some reason, the judge seemed prejudiced against him and did whatever he could to break him down in both, body and spirit. He hadn't even allowed anyone but his attorney to come see him until after the trial was over.

He heard a noise and looked toward the door of his cell and saw two guards, one with a rifle standing a few steps to the side while the other guard opened the door and brought in a bowl of mush and a cup of lukewarm coffee and set it on Clay's bunk.

"That's not the evenin' meal I'm supposed ta get," Clay said. "Where's the food from the restaurant?"

"Well, ya see, it's like this," he said with a grin, "me and Ike, over there," he motioned with his hand, indicating the other guard. "We ate it. And it was almighty good, too."

Ike, the guard with the rifle spoke up. "Now that the senora ain't here no more, you'll be eatin' mush, again. And if'n that lady from the restaurant keeps comin' over with food like she brung taday, well now, me and Luke, there, we jest might put on a pound'er two afore you go off ta Huntsville ta get yer neck stretched. And don't think yer lawyer man can do anything, either. I hear the judge ain't speakin' to him."

Luke closed the cell door and locked it, and as he walked away, he said, "No matter, anyway. Looks like you and two others will be makin' the trip ta Huntsville, real soon like."

"Three of us?" Clay asked. He was the only one in the cellblock that he knew of.

"Yep," Luke said. "They got ah couple of horse thieves over to the city jail and the judge, he sentenced them ta hang right alongside you. He sure do like seein' men get hung."

Ike punched Luke in the ribs with his elbow. "Sure wish the judge'd build us ah gallows ta use here in Austin. Hell, I'd pull the lever."

"Probably draw ah big crowd, too. Hangin's can be ah right popular event."

Clay watched them leave and felt a chill run down his spine. How much time did he have left before they took him to Huntsville, he wondered as he drank the lukewarm coffee. He decided against the mush. He'd just gotten used to eating real food again and mush was a poor substitute. "You'd think they'd let ah man at least eat a few decent meals before they hang him," he said to the empty room.

Later that same evening, after a very tasty French dinner Abigail had concocted, Horatio B. Tyson sat back on the couch, sipping on a glass of imported champagne and enjoying a cigar while she cleaned up the dishes. He was envisioning what the night would be like a little later on. Abigail had a voracious appetite in the bedroom and for the time being, he would enjoy her company. And, if things worked out, Matilda Johnston might be added to his list of lady friends. Her husband had been gone for five years and she had recently inquired if the court could declare him legally dead. She had that look about her he'd come to recognize. He truly did love widow women.

His thoughts were interrupted by Abigail, who sat down next to him and kissed him on the cheek. "I was just wondering if you'd decided when you were going to send those three awful men to Huntsville?"

"Funny you should ask," Horatio said, blowing a cloud of smoke into the room. "I was just sitting here thinking about that very thing." Telling her lies was getting easier and easier; she was so gullible. She believed anything he told her.

"And did you decide on a date?" she asked, nibbling on his ear.

She was up to something, he thought to himself. He'd just play along and see what she was up to. "I'm thinking about one day next week. I telegraphed the warden and he said I could send them any time," which was the truth, but he'd been busy and didn't see the rush, so he let them sit here in his jail and stew. Being hung could be very troublesome on the mind.

"When would the actual hanging be done? Right away? Or will the warden over there make them wait?"

Did he detect a gleam in her eyes? Was she getting excited about getting a man hung?

"Oh, I don't know. I guess that would be up to the warden. Although, I guess I could set a date. It is within my power, you know."

Abigail ran her hand inside his shirt and began to gently rub his chest. "Do you suppose we could be there to see it? As witnesses. After all, it was me who brought the complaint against Mister Brentwood and you were the judge who sentenced him. I mean it does stand to reason that we should be the ones to witness justice being done."

Her breath was now coming in ragged gasps and her eyes looked all glazed over.

"I see no reason why we can't," he said, just before she kissed him with a greater passion than ever before.

Standing, she took him by the hand and led him to her bedroom.

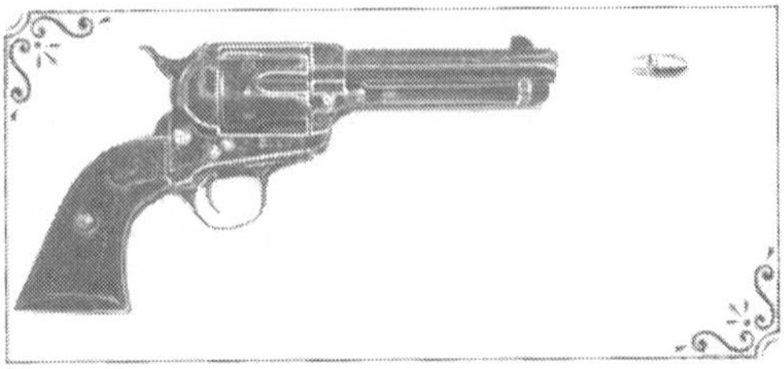

# CHAPTER ELEVEN

-

The two horse thieves, Jake Comers and Julio Flores, were also wondering when they were going to be transferred to Huntsville, but with a different reason in mind. Their plans did not include being hung at Huntsville, or anyplace else, for that matter.

They knew the route the prison wagon would take and their plan was set. A man Jake knew sneaked up to the window a few nights ago and a plan for their escape had been worked out. They knew how, just not, when.

“What about this gringo who is over in the county jail? I hear he is a very bad man who kills people just for smiling at him wrong. Do you think that is true?” Julio asked.

“Don’t know.” Jake Comers said shaking his head from side to side. “But, if he is, we might just be able to fit him into our plan. If we play our cards right, he could wind up the scapegoat and we'd be off, scot-free… Hell, the way I heard it, he's killed at least twenty men or maybe more, already."

Julio smiled. "Amigo, you have a devious mind."

"If that means what I think it means, you're right," Jake said walking over and looking out of the window in the direction of the county jail. To his left, he saw what looked like someone lighting a cigarette and turned his head to stare in that direction. After a moment, he saw a small glow moving back and forth. He waved his hand in front of the window until he saw the small glow disappear.

"I'm gonna have ah visitor this evenin'," he whispered to Julio who looked toward the window but saw nothing. "He'll be bringin' us information on that man over in the county jail. You keep watch while I talk with him."

Julio nodded his head.

Lying on their bunks, pretending to be asleep, they waited for the visitor. It was about midnight or a little after when a pebble was thrown through the barred window and rattled across the floor.

Jake swung his legs over the side of the bunk, stood up and looked around. When he saw no guards anywhere near, he nodded at Julio, then walked over to the window and began to whisper to someone standing outside.

Julio eased out of bed and kept his eyes on the doorway leading to where the guards stayed. In his hand, was a knife taken from its hiding place in his right boot. He held the knife down low, close to his right leg.

After standing watch for about five minutes, he heard the sound of a key turning in the door leading to their cells. Turning quickly, he made a, "psst," sound as he slid into his bunk and pretended to be asleep.

The door opened and one of the guards walked down along the cells shining a lantern into each cell, checking to make sure the prisoners were in their bunks asleep. When he got to Julio and Jake's cell, he noticed one of the bunks was empty and began to shine the light around the inside of the cell.

"Hey, can't a man get some privacy around here?"

The guard swung the light a little farther and found Jake sitting on the slop bucket with his pants down.

"Sorry," he said and turned and went back to the guard's quarters.

Julio snickered under his breath as he watched Jake pull his pants up and go back to the window.

Julio decided not to stand up this time. He swung his legs over the side of the bunk and sat up. He could see all he needed to see from that position. Plus, he could get back in bed faster if the guard came back. He wished Jake would hurry up - he was getting sleepy.

A few minutes later, Jake returned and crawled onto his bunk and lit a cigar. "Seems like that fella over in the county jail, that Clay Brentwood, is ah rich man. Has ah good size ranch up north of here ah ways and owns several businesses and ah bank, up in Wichita. And even with all that money, he's still gonna hang. Not me. I would have bought my freedom."

Julio let out a low whistle. "Are you thinking what I am thinking, mi amigo?"

"If you're thinkin' we could wind up ownin' ah ranch and havin' money ta stock it with, then we're thinkin' the same thing."

Julio put his hands under his head and stretched out on his bunk, dreaming of being a rich landowner with many senoritas to cook his meals and take care of him. He would have thousands of cows, and fine bred horses to ride.

Jake was also thinking of his future, but in his dream, he was using his share of the money to travel the world and in each country, he had a different woman on his arm.

Julio could have the ranch. He would take the bank and all the money it made.

As the moon moved toward the western horizon, Howard Loring sat with his head on his desk, facing toward the wall; an open book next to his head - his snores ruffling the pages of the book as the lamp flickered and went out.

Clay was the only one still awake – standing next to the window, staring out at the moon. "If you're really up there, God, which I'm not so sure about any more, I'm told you're ah forgivin' God. If that's true, why haven't you forgiven me? I admit I've killed.  And the good book says you frown on that sort of thing; but I only killed bad men – you know, an eye for an eye, or men who were tryin' ta kill me or tryin' ta help innocent folks who couldn't defend themselves."

Except for the rain, the night was quiet, and after a while, Clay turned and walked over and laid down on his bunk, staring at the ceiling while he waited for morning and a cup of lukewarm coffee, wondering how his life would have been if he hadn't gone after Curly and his gang? For sure, he wouldn't be layin' here on this bunk, waitin' to get his neck stretched.

But if he hadn't gone after Curly and his gang, how many other people would have died? Maybe that was the price – his life in place of all those who wouldn't have been killed by Curly and the hard-cases who rode with him.

He wasn't afraid to die; it happened to everbody. He just hadn't planned on it bein' this soon or dyin' at the end of a rope.

Clay could see the moon shining through the window of his cell. "Well, Martha," he said to the moon, "I may come to see you ah mite sooner than I'd planned on."

Folding his hands under the back of his head, he closed his eyes and was soon asleep.

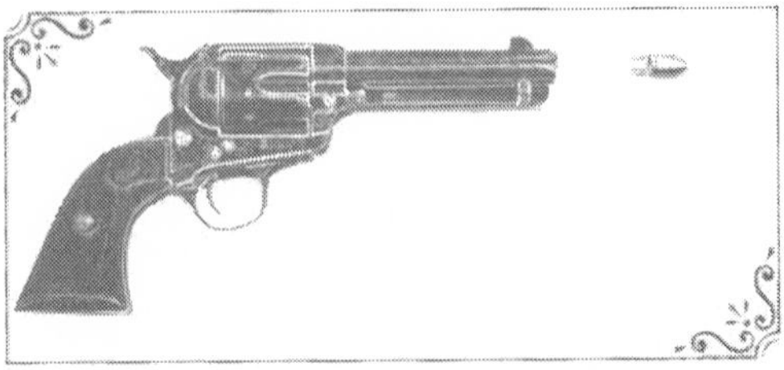

# CHAPTER TWELVE

After a leisurely breakfast, Judge Tyson kissed Abigail and slipped out the back door of her house and went directly to his apartment where he bathed, put on a clean suit, and then went to the courthouse. She had convinced him it was time to send the prisoners to Huntsville to be executed.

"Sitting here in the jails, they are just wasting the city and county's money to feed and house them when it should be the state's worry," she'd told him in her matter of fact tone.

Sitting behind his desk, waiting for his bailiff to arrive, he had to agree with her sense of logic. Besides, he was getting tired of that mouthpiece, Howard Loring, always pestering him and trying to get an audience with the governor, whom he had taken great pains to make sure wouldn't happen. In his eyes, the governor was a weak man who didn't deserve the position he held. He let his mind drift… maybe one day he would be seated in the governor's chair – and when that day came, they would have no doubt who was in charge.

When the bailiff, Henry Potts, a cowardly sort of man who was deathly afraid of the judge, and with good reason, arrived, the judge instructed him to fetch the city marshal to his office post haste.

As Henry raced away to do the judge's bidding, the judge chuckled to himself. He had Henry under his thumb because he made the man believe he could still send him to the gallows for something that happened five years ago – which in reality, had been an accident and he had no jurisdiction, but Henry Potts didn't know that.

The horse pulling Henry's buggy had shied when a young boy threw a firecracker under the horse's feet during a Fourth of July festival, up in Missouri. The wagon tipped over, killing the boy. The judge up there had ruled it an accident and had set him free, but the judge convinced Henry it didn't make any difference. He told Henry he could re-open the case any time he wanted to and could sentence him to hang - stating that Henry should have had better control over the horse, and therefore guilty of second degree murder. He explained in great detail there was no limitation on murder, even one that had been decided on in court - and of course, Henry believed him. After all, he was a judge and Henry was just a lowly clerk.

The city marshal, Clive Werner, was actually an ex-outlaw turned lawman to keep from going to jail. In Kansas and Oklahoma, he had done some cattle rustling and had shot a man over a poker debt. When he arrived in Austin, they were looking for someone to take the job of city marshal and weren't having much success. The last two marshals had been shot down by a Mexican hard case that was known only as, Diablo.

Clive Werner called Diablo out and shot him down in the middle of the street, and then walked into the mayor's office and applied for the job of city marshal. He was hired on the spot. That had been two and a half years ago.

At six feet three inches, he towered over most of the men he went up against and he had a look about him that broached no nonsense. And even though he wasn't what might be called, a fast gun, he was fast enough and hit what he shot at. But most of the time he didn't have to draw his pistol. He carried a leather pouch filled with lead and he would walk up to the man, hit him on the head, knock him out; and when the man woke up, he was in jail.

Twenty minutes after being summoned, the marshal sauntered into the judge's chambers and looked down at him. He didn't particularly like the judge but didn't know why. There was just something about the man that caused the hackles on his neck to rise.

"You wanted to see me?" he asked as he dropped into the chair in front of the judge's desk, throwing his leg over his knee in a casual, laid back manner.

Judge Tyson stared with contempt at the arrogance of this man – sitting down without out being asked, and in such a vulgar manner. 'I will do some research on this insolent piece of trash who struts around town like he owns the world,' he thought to himself.

"Yes. I have decided to send the three prisoners to Huntsville today, and I want you to see to it."

"I'll need something in writing," the marshal said in an off-handed manner.

The judge slid a piece of paper across the desk toward the marshal. "You can pick your own driver and guards, but I want the best you have. And have one of them deliver this second piece of paper to the warden at Huntsville. It contains the day I want them executed," the judge said, waving his hand in dismissal as he opened a law book.

Clive Werner stood up slowly, glaring down at the judge. "Will that be all?"

"For now," the judge said, not even looking up.

The marshal turned and headed for the door, muttering under his breath, "How you got to be a judge is beyond me."

Judge Tyson was too absorbed in what he was doing to even notice the snide remark.

Once he was alone, he leaned back in his chair, wondering what it would take for him to become governor. He was sure he could do a better job than that idiot up there now.

As the marshal was walking down the steps leading from the courthouse, he passed Abigail Schuster coming up the steps. She looked at him with a seductive smile that made a shiver run down his back. Everybody in town knew about her and the judge. Besides, she wasn't his type.

He tipped his hat and hurried down the street in the direction of the livery stable where the prison wagon was kept.

An hour later, the two prisoners from the city jail were led out, unencumbered by shackles or handcuffs, and put into the prison wagon. The wagon then proceeded over to the county jail, where Clay was led out to the wagon. People stopped to stare at him and make whispered comments.

It was all he could do to shuffle along, shackled in leg irons. Unlike the rustlers, who had no restraints, Clay's wrists were handcuffed behind him, making it hard to keep his balance.

Bull Anderson and Terrance Billings had been chosen to make the trip as guards because of their past experience. Both men carried double-barreled shotguns. Terrance Billings pointed his shotgun through the bars at the two men from the city jail, while Bull Anderson shoved Clay through the open door of the prison wagon, then slammed and padlocked the door once he was inside, as if Clay was some monster to be feared.

Clay landed face down on the floor of the wagon and was struggling to get up. Both, Jake Comers and Julio Flores reached out and grabbed an arm, helping Clay to his feet.

"Thanks," he said, sitting down on the bench and leaning back against the bars, looking around. "You'd think if this is supposed ta be our last ride, they could've at least given us soft seats ta ride on," Clay said with a grin, as the wagon jerked and started down the street. Hank Slope, the driver, was fifteen minutes behind schedule, was in a bad mood and had a hangover. He didn't like his job, but driving a team was what he did. He had only taken this assignment because he was broke. As the driver of the prison wagon, it paid more than driving other kinds of wagons.

One of the guards, Terrance Billings, rode up front with Hank. He was a small man with evil eyes and a sour disposition. The other guard, Bull Anderson, was like a small bull, stout but not fat, and he loved a good fight. Bull stretched out in a prone position on top where he could keep an eye on the surrounding area as they rolled down the road. He hoped there wouldn't be any trouble, but Bull was the kind of man who didn't like taking chances, especially when his life might be at stake. His beady eyes scanned the people standing on the sidewalks, gawking, as the prison wagon went by. In Bull's way of thinking, everyone was suspect. Fortunately, no one tested Bull's ability with the shotgun.

Howard Loring was headed for the judge's chambers to once again try to reason with the man, when he saw the prison wagon come rolling down the street. He stopped and looked at it as it went past. When he saw Clay inside, trussed up like a threat to society, he ran out into the street, yelling, "Hey, stop! Stop! That's my client in there! You can't…"

Hank barely glanced at the young lawyer running alongside the wagon, as he flicked the reins against the horse's rumps and picked up speed. He had no time for lawyers. He had a headache and he'd been given a schedule he intended to keep, if it was within his power. The sooner he could get his prisoners to Huntsville, the sooner he could find a jug and a woman to snuggle up to.

Howard watched the departing prison wagon for only a moment, then changed his mind about going to see the judge and headed for the ranger's office, which was only a few doors down – a new idea was forming in his mind.

At the ranger's office, he was informed that Bill McDaniel was out of town and not expected back for a few more days. Frustrated and dejected, Howard Loring went back to his office and wrote down some of the things he wanted to talk to the ranger about.

The prison wagon rolled east out of Austin and headed for Huntsville at a brisk pace. The land was barren and dry, as was that part of Texas. Dust boiled up from the road filling the inside of the wagon, causing the prisoners to cough. They did little but cough and try to breathe with their shirtsleeves up against their noses. There were no walls to keep out the weather, only steel bars, and because of that, the prisoners suffered from the heat and the dust.

At the instruction of Bull Anderson, earlier, there was to be no talking amongst the prisoners, which was not a problem. With all the dust choking them, they were in no mood to talk.

Just before the sun disappeared behind the far hills, Hank Slope pulled the wagon off the main road and followed a trail that was no more than two ruts, for about a quarter of a mile. In a cluster of boulders, there was a small pond of water. It was a place he'd used before, as had others, which was evidenced by a fire pit that looked like it had held many fires. Nearby, someone had left a small pile of wood and a bit of dried grass, which made a good fire starter.

The prisoners were led from the wagon and each tied in a sitting position to a different wagon wheel so he could eat. His arms were free, but not within range to reach the knots that bound him, which were tied to hooks sticking out from the cross member under the wagon. With a shotgun cradled across his arms, Terrance informed them they would remain tied to the wagon wheel throughout the night.

Jake Comers bristled up and shouted, “That means we’ll half’ta sleep sitting up and I don’t do that none too good. Can’t you at least give us some slack so we can lay down?”

Clay watched the hard eyes of Terrance dance and the sly grin on his unshaven face. The man was enjoying his control over them. He’d read somewhere about small men and their lust for power over others, and here was a prime example.

“Sleep or don’t sleep – makes no difference to me,” Terrance said as he walked toward the fire pit and the coffee pot.

During supper, Clay decided that at least they ate better than the normal fare in the county jail, where it had been mush and lukewarm coffee. Here, he was given hot coffee and there was bacon and beans to eat, with some hardtack, which he dipped in his coffee to soften it up some.

The sky was overcast and turned dark, early. It would rain before morning and Clay liked the idea that he would be left outside, which would allow the rain to wash off some of the dust that was clogging his nose and eyes and clinging to his clothes. He just hoped it wouldn’t turn cold.

Of course, he had no such luck. When the rain started and it looked to be a gully washer, they were hustled back inside the wagon, which didn’t do a lot of good, except from overhead. The wind blew rain through the bars on the sides and soaked them anyway, and the temperature dropped dramatically. All they could do was sit there and try to endure wet and cold. Clay's teeth chattered so loud he thought they might break.

With the prisoners locked inside the wagon, the guards could relax and didn't have to stand watch. Instead, they sat huddled under the lean-to tarpaulin that had been erected by Hank, with a small fire just inside to keep them and the coffee, warm. Hank had made this run before and had encountered a rainstorm or two. This time, he was prepared.

The lean-to was some twenty yards from the wagon, nestled in among some elm trees to help shelter it from the rain, and far enough away so that whispered voices of the prisoners couldn't be heard over the storm.

"Sure would be nice if we could somehow get loose before we get to Huntsville," Jake Comers said in a low voice, talking to Julio, but loud enough for Clay to hear.

"Si, I would give mucho dinero, if I had any, to get free. I am too young to die. There will be many senoritas who will cry when I'm gone."

"Way I hear it; these guards are too afraid of Judge Tyson to take bribe money. So, even if we had any, it wouldn't do us much good," Jake whispered, sneaking a peak at Clay to see if he was listening.

The whole thing had been planned out and rehearsed back in the city jail. They had just been waiting for the right time to test the water, so to speak.

"I do not know, mi amigo. You give a man enough dinero and he will think hard about it. There are a lot of places he could go where the judge would never find him. He could even go south to the gulf and catch a ship out of the country. But, of course, he would have to have gold or silver, and a lot of it."

Clay sat with his head bowed low, pretending to sleep. He grinned slightly at their crude attempt to con him. They must have somehow found out that he had money. Probably heard the guards talking. They were known to have loose jaws. No matter. He was wondering what their game was, and decided to play along, at least for the time being.

"How much gold do you think it might take to get us free?" he asked without raising his head.

"More than any of us has," Jake responded. "That is, unless you're rich," he whispered with a chuckle.

Julio leaned in close to Clay and asked, "Are you rich, Senor'?"

"Might be able to lay my hands on some money, but I'd have to be free and be able to go up north, cause that's where I'd have ta go ta get it. But none of that means a hill of beans, now does it? You boys are talkin' about havin' money in our pockets that we can fork over right now. Right?"

"If I had ah large chunk of money in a bank up north, I just might be able to strike up a deal with them," Jake said as he leaned back against the bars and closed his eyes, pretending to sleep.

Clay knew they were up to something, but at this point he wasn't sure what it might be. Could they really talk the guards into setting them free, for a price? If they couldn't, the only other possibility would be an escape attempt. But how they would they go about it, he didn't know. He would just have to be patient. From what little he'd seen of him, Jake looked to be a con man and he had a plan, of that he was sure. Whatever his plan was, it would have to be acted on soon; Huntsville was no more than two days to the east.

Clay wanted to be free, but he didn't want to kill anyone to do it. The men guardin' them were just doin' a job, and not makin' much money for it either. Killin' them would mean he would be a hunted man and on the run for the rest of his life. On the other hand, he didn't want to hang, either. Giving a sigh, he decided to try to get some sleep; tomorrow might be an interesting day and he would deal with things as they came along.

Jake Comers was not asleep, but sitting quietly, remembering his days in Kansas City as a shoulder striker for Big Mike Lombroski. At least, that's how he'd thought of himself in those days. But truth be told, he had been nothing more than a small-time collector, picking up bags of money owed to Big Mike. Because he worked for Big Mike, he could push his weight around and get away with it, which he did. It was only tolerated because of who his boss was, and no one was really afraid of him. Once, after watching a poker game, he'd shot a man in the back and stole his winnings. He'd gotten away with it, but knew he'd never have what it took to stand face to face with a man and shoot it out like Big Mike would.

Big Mike was a bone breaker when he was crossed or when somebody tried to come down on one of his boys, he made sure they never did it again. At least twenty men he knew of had disappeared – never to be seen or heard of again. And then a few weeks later, Big Mike would come up with the signed deed to their business or property and take it over. He was a rich man and nobody could prove a thing against him. Big Mike was smart – at least that's the way Jake saw it.

A few days after shooting the man in the back, Jake heard the law knocking on his door and he'd run like a scared rabbit and found out six months later, it had nothing to do with the shooting, they just wanted him to buy some tickets to an affair they were putting on.

Six days after leaving Kansas City, he wound up in Texas, broke and hungry. In a bar, he threw in with some men bent on robbing the local bank.

Jake was introduced to a man wearing a business suit. The man had not given his name, but only nodded at him. Jake had no doubt this man was the boss.

Being new to the gang, he was given the job of holding the getaway horses, which he did, but his take only amounted to thirteen dollars, which irritated him because the rest all made a lot more.

The next day, Jake left the gang and was riding south across the vast plains of southern Texas when he saw a large herd of cattle and got an idea. He figured he was only a few miles from the Mexican border and if he took a few beeves down to Mexico and sold them, no one would be the wiser. The herd, being as big as it was, it would be easy work and they probably wouldn't even be missed. Nobody around this part of the country knew him and he was sure he'd find a buyer down in Mexico in a matter of days.

It had worked smooth as butter and he had what he considered, a new career - one that put easy money in his pocket. In a saloon down in Mexico, he met Julio, who at the time was drifting and looking for work. They struck up a friendship and Jake offered Julio a partnership. Julio wasn't sure. Stealing cattle was a hanging offense, but Jake convinced him no one would catch them, and moving cattle with two riders made the work easier and they could more than double the amount of cows they stole.

The only problem was, Jake didn't have sense enough to choose a different rancher each time they went to steal cattle, and on the fifth trip to the same rancher, he found the owner and his men, waiting on him. They were lucky they didn't get strung up right then and there. The only reason they weren't was because the city marshal was with them and talked the owner into turning them over to him. And now, here they were, on the road to the prison in Huntsville where they would be hung.

Fortunately, as far as Jake was concerned, one of the outlaws from the old gang he'd ridden with during the bank robbery, just happened to be coming out of the saloon in Austin and saw the law bringing him in. Later, the man had slipped up to the window and after some talk, a plan for his escape began to form. Of course, he'd had to promise the man a sizeable amount of money, which he didn't have, but now as he understood it, Clay Brentwood, the one they had over in the county jail, did, and it was his intention to get his hands on Clay's fortune.

Julio was also doing some thinking. He was wishing he'd never met up with Jake and allowing himself to be talked into rustling cows. He knew he could have made it as a cowboy. He could ride, and rope; and he knew cattle. All he'd needed was a little money to buy himself a good horse and rig. He'd gotten greedy - hungry for money, and because of it, in a few days, long before he'd had a chance to live, he would be dead.

Early the next morning, Hank Slope had everyone awake – a small amount of bacon and one cup of coffee was all they had before the prison wagon headed east at a goodly pace.

The rain seemed to bother Hank Slope a lot, Clay thought as the wagon jostled him around on the seat. He thought he'd heard Hank say something about the Brazos River flooding with all this rain and he wanted to be on the east side of the river before it did.

Clay searched his mind. He'd read somethin' about this Brazos River, which was not too far east of his place up north. What was it? Oh yeah, it was eight hundred and forty miles long and came down from the Black Water draw and ran all the way to the ocean.

The article said somethin' about the river beginnin' at the confluence of the Salt Fork and the Double Mountain and emptyin' into the marshes just south of Freeport, Texas, where it connected with the Gulf of Mexico. The article also said the river was subject to heavy floodin' during the rainy season and went on to say that it was often confused by easterners who called it the Colorado River, which was still some forty-five or fifty miles west of where they were now.

Tryin' ta cross the river while it was flooded would be dangerous. Flooded rivers could have a mighty strong current, which might turn the prison wagon over. And if that happened, with the door bein' padlocked, there would be no way for them to escape and they would drown. And even if they could get out, bein' handcuffed and in shackles, he wasn't sure he could swim carrying all that extra weight, especially against a strong current.

"You don't suppose they'll try ta cross the river if it's flooded, do ya?" Clay asked.

Jake looked up and said, "I don't think they'd be that stupid, but you never know. If they have to wait on this side, it might take a couple of days or more for the river to go down enough so's they can cross.

"But on the other hand, if they don't get us delivered to Huntsville by sometime tomorrow, the judge ain't gonna be happy. Me, I could care less about what the judge thinks, but I'll bet it's worrying those three men out there. The truth is, I ain't worried cause there just might be a third choice."

"What's that supposed to mean?" Clay asked.

Jake grinned and said, "If I was you, Mister Brentwood, I'd get as much rest as I could, you just might need it real soon like."

With that, Jake pulled his hat down over his eyes and leaned his back against the bars of the prison wagon and promptly went to sleep.

Clay allowed what Jake said to bounce around inside his head, trying to figure out what he meant by his last statement, and the only conclusion he could come up with was an escape plan of some kind. Had he paid off the driver, or one of the guards - or maybe all three? He had said something earlier about bribing them with gold or silver.

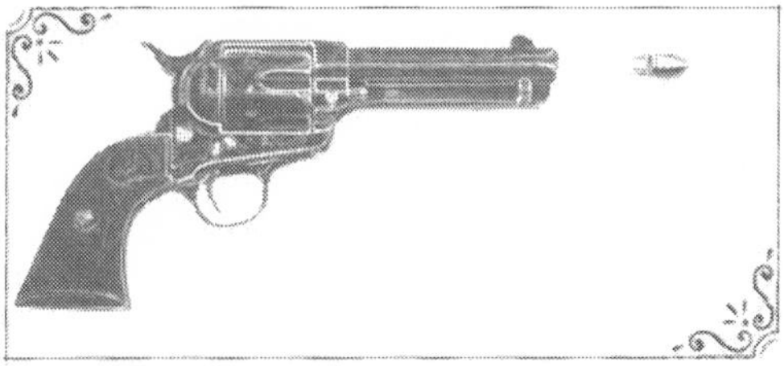

# CHAPTER THIRTEEN

-

There was a scattering of cottonwood trees lining both sides of the Brazos River where the road ended. There had been talk of building a bridge, but that was as far as it got. During normal times, getting across the river was not usually a problem, but when it flooded, crossing on horseback or in a wagon, was out of the question and swimming it was impossible.

Hank Slope pulled back on the reins and brought the horses to a stop and swore. They were too late. The river was several feet over its banks on both sides and running fast – way too fast to cross. Neither man nor horse could swim against that current.

"I was afraid of this," Hank said, shaking his head. "Guess there ain't much we can do but wait til it goes down. Might as well make camp, we're apt to be here for a day or two."

"Sounds okay by me," Bull said. "I could use a cup or two of more coffee and seeing as how we didn't have much of a breakfast, some biscuits and gravy might taste real good about now."

Bull was of a rotund nature and hated to miss many meals. He figured if they were to be here a day or so, why not catch up on some rest and maybe have an extra meal or two. His stomach had been growling from a lack of sustenance.

Although Terrance Billings would not turn down some biscuits and gravy, just coffee would have suited him just fine. Being short and wiry, he didn't need as much food as Bull did, but he had to admit, Hank bein' in such ah hurry and all, they had been eatin' kinda light.

At the same time Hank decided to make camp next to the flooded river, Howard Loring was sitting on a chair near the front door of the livery stable, watching the street. He was waiting for Bill McDaniel to show up. And when finally, he did, he hustled Bill over to a nearby restaurant so they could talk. Over supper, he brought him up to date on what had happened and offered up the plan he had in mind to keep Clay from getting hung.

The ranger finished his steak, and as he sat eating the piece of mincemeat pie that came with his coffee, he said, “You know, Howard, that just might work.”

Howard smiled for the first time in a long while, hoping they could pull it off before it was too late.

“Alright, everybody out,” Bull yelled as he unlocked the door of the prison wagon. “You two,” he said to Jake and Julio, “you can start making a camp. And you, Brentwood, you gather firewood. And don’t forget to get some small stuff ta start the fire with.”

Clay shuffled off towards the woods, wondering how he could gather wood all trussed up like he was. Bull called after him, “and don’t you be gettin’ no ideas about runnin’. First off, there ain’t no place ta go. And second, Terrance will have his shotgun trained on your back. You can try to swim the river if you want, but I wouldn’t advise it, not with all that extra weight you’re carryin’.” Bull walked away laughing at his joke.

Clay moved as quickly as he could, which wasn’t very fast with shackles on his legs. He found some dry downfall and small branches. He had wandered a good ways back into the forest, looking for tender to use for starting the fire, when he saw the men standing next to their horses. They stood holding their hands over the horse's noses so they wouldn't make any noise. He counted six, hard looking men. One of them placed his finger against his lips, indicating Clay be quiet.

Clay glanced over his shoulder and noticed Terrance had stopped to roll and light a cigarette. His head was bowed and couldn't see the men just beyond where Clay was standing.

"So that's what Jake had meant when he said to get some rest," Clay whispered to himself. If these men are here to help us escape, they couldn't have planned it any better. Hank and the guards would be looking forward to coffee and something to eat, unaware that all hell was about to break loose and their lives were about to come to an abrupt end. It would be like shootin' ducks at one of them shootin' galleries, then hard ridin' to get well away before anyone found out about it. Hell, they could even shove the wagon into the river and folks might think it had turned over and everbody had drowned.

Clay stood there, his mind in a quandary. Should he yell out, he wondered? If I do, I will more than likely be dead before the men in the camp could react; but lettin' them get murdered without a chance to defend themselves, wasn't right either.

He heard a slight gasp and looked back in Terrance's direction just in time to see him slump to the ground. A tall man, wearing buckskins, moccasins and had a feather hanging in his long black hair was standing next to him, a knife in his hand. There was blood dripping from the blade. He was an Indian, but Clay wasn't sure what tribe.

One by one the outlaws moved past him quietly - heading toward the camp. They had pistols in their fists, and as they passed, they each handed him the reins of his horse. Without being asked or wanting to, Clay Brentwood suddenly became part of the slaughter that was about to take place. By holding their horses, he had just become a member of their gang and was, in the eyes of the law, guilty by association.

Thinking he could swing onto the back of one of the horses and sprint away, Clay was about to take a chance and yell out, hoping to at least give them a chance to defend themselves. But before he could act, the man who had killed Terrance came out of nowhere and eased up next to him. Clay felt the tip of the knife gently prick the skin just under his ribs on the left side.

"Preciate it if you don't make any noise til it's over, then you can yell all you want to cause you'll be ah free man. And knowin' your neck ain't gonna get stretched... well, the boss, he figures that might be worth something."

So that was it, Clay thought. They help me escape and figure I'll take them up to Wichita and open the door to the bank and let'em have what they want.

Suddenly, the air was filled with gunfire and the smell of gunpowder. Clay looked in the direction of the camp and felt a lump in his throat. The outlaws had given them no warning. They'd just sauntered in real quiet like and cut loose.

Sure enough, when he and the tall man in the moccasins walked into camp, both Bull and Hank were lying on the ground, riddled with bullet wounds, blood seeping out of them, making small puddles on the ground.

A man dressed in a dirty, but expensive looking suit, glanced at Jake and Julio and said, "Drag'em over to the river and toss'em in. As fast as the river is flowin' they'll be shark bait in the ocean before anyone knows they're gone."

One of the outlaws came walking into camp, his arms loaded with the wood Clay had gathered. Clay didn't remember doing it, but he must have dropped the wood when he saw Terrance being murdered. Seeing a man get murdered like that, in cold blood, could cause a fella to forget what he was doing.

The man in the suit looked around, and then asked, "Wasn't there three of 'em? Where's the other one?"

"He's back in the trees where the Kiowa left him," the outlaw with the wood said, as he dropped the firewood onto the ground and began to build a fire.

"Well, don't just leave him there. Somebody drag his carcass down to the river and throw him in! God, do I have to think of everything?"

Turning, he looked at the tall Indian. "Kiowa, you killed him, so you drag him down to the river. I don't want any bodies, or that wagon, left behind."

The tall Indian stared at the man in the suit for just a moment and the look in his eyes made the hair on the back of Clay's neck stand on end. God, he has mean lookin' eyes, Clay thought. Then, without a word, the Indian turned and walked into the forest.

While the beans were heating, bacon was frying, and the coffee was brewing, the man in the suit took a set of keys that he found hanging near the driver's seat of the prison wagon and unlocked Clay's handcuffs and leg irons, setting him free.

"You're a free man, Mister Brentwood, or will be as soon as you pay us for this act of kindness."

Clay rubbed his wrists and shook his head. "You expect me to pay you for killin' these men, just so I could go free?"

"That's about the size of it," the man in the suit said. "I can't take all the credit; it was Jake's idea to do it. I just figured out the when and the how."

"And how much will those two be payin'?" Clay asked, pointing at Jake and Julio.

The man in the suit poured himself a cup of coffee, blew on it, and then took a sip. "Don't guess that is any concern of yours. Your only concern is your own neck, and if you don't feel obligated to compensate us for saving your life, then I guess we can have us a necktie party right here under one of these lovely cottonwood trees, or we could handcuff you and put those shackles back on your ankles and throw you in the river. It makes no difference to me."

"Really?" Clay said. "Makes no difference to you that you'd go ta all this trouble and not get anything out of it except the pleasure of killin' a man you don't even know?"

The man in the suit took another sip of his coffee, looking at Clay over the rim of the cup. When he finished, a quick movement of his hand sent hot coffee into Clay's face.

Clay jumped back and reacted by brushing the coffee from his face and shirt. "What the hell did you do that for?" he yelled.

"I forgot to mention," the man in the suit said, "Before we hang you, or throw you in the river, we'll have us a bit of fun to see how tough you are. Kiowa, being an Indian, knows a great many ways to break a man down – like skinning a man alive, just a few inches at a time, or hanging him by his thumbs from a tree limb and lighting a fire under his bare feet. You'd be begging us to take your money. The hot coffee was just to get your attention so I could explain what you'll be in for if you decide not to pay us our just due."

Clay looked over at Jake and Julio, who were standing just off to the side. Jake had a smirk on his face and his eyes were dancing with excitement, while Julio had a look of remorse and stared at his feet.

"So, this was your idea, was it?" Clay asked Jake, who tucked his thumbs in his belt and swelled up his chest.

"It was," Jake said with a bit of bravado. "Word is, your ah rich man with plenty to share, and me and the boys being without funds at the present time, could help you spend some of it. Saving your neck should be worth quite a lot to a man rich as you."

"You figured that out, all by yourself, did you?" Clay asked and watched as Jake shook his head, a wide grin on his face.

"Well think about this, smart guy. When this is all over, you're the first one I'm gonna come lookin' for."

Clay watched the smirk fade and his jaw drop. He hadn't thought about that.

"Enough of this chit-chat," the man in the suit said. "Do we have a deal, or do I let the Kiowa open the torture dance?"

Clay knew if he didn't play along with them he was a dead man, and he wasn't ready to die. If, on the other hand, he pretended to go along with them, they might make a mistake somewhere along the line and give him an opportunity to somehow get out of this mess.

"Well now, Mister… I didn't catch your name and I hate doin' business with a man whose name I don't know," Clay said, almost apologetic. It was obvious that he was dealing with a self-centered man who thought more of himself than he had a right to.

The man in the suit had just poured himself a fresh cup of coffee and turned to face Clay. "Aaron. The name's Aaron; Aaron Hammershield. Most folks call me," The Hammer." But you can call me, Mister Hammershield. Now, about our reward for setting you free."

Clay wiped his hand across his mouth. "I reckon I could talk business better if I had some coffee and maybe a chunk or two of that bacon, and maybe ah plate of beans to go along with the bacon. It's been awhile."

"Help yourself, Mister Brentwood," Hammershield said, waving his arm in a wide hospitable gesture.

After a cup of coffee, a plate of beans, and several slices of bacon, Clay walked over and sat down next to Aaron Hammershield.

The man was smoking one of those handmade cigarillos and offered one to Clay. "Man down in Mexico City makes them. I find them much better than the ones you get up here."

Clay took the cigarillo and lit it with the stick match offered by Hammershield, and after a few puffs, he asked, "How much of a reward are you thinkin' I should pay, Mister Hammershield?"

Hammershield thought for a minute while he blew smoke rings into the air. "That will depend on how much you have, Mister Brentwood. I would need to see your bank book and investment records."

This man was not some two-bit hustler, Clay thought to himself. He was a thinker and conniver and he would need to be strong when dealing with him or the man would see right through him. "Well now, ta do that, I reckon we'll need ta go up ta

Wichita. That's where that information is, and truth be told, I don't have ah clue as to how much I'm worth; all the paperwork is handled by an attorney up there. But if we can settle on an amount, maybe I could write you a check if you've got a pencil and piece of paper."

Aaron Hammershield threw his head back and laughed so hard it caused him to snort. When he was finally able to calm down, he looked at Clay and said, "You are funny, my friend. Yes, very funny indeed.  Write me a check. I think not. Gold or silver is what I want, not a check or any of that paper money. Gold or silver is something we can spend anywhere. No one questions silver or gold, my friend."

"Then I reckon we'll just have ta go up ta Wichita," Clay said with an innocent smile. His assumption was correct; this was not some greedy fool to be suckered into a simple ruse like writing a worthless check.

# CHAPTER FOURTEEN

-

The following morning, they cleaned up the campsite to look like it hadn't been used in some time. With the bodies washed away with the current, there was only one more chore to do, and that was to make it look like the wagon had been driven into the river.

Clay smiled as he watched the final details. Bushy limbs had been used to brush away any tracks except the ones of the wagon wheels and the hoof prints of six draft horses. One of the outlaws hitched the horses to the wagon and took it back up the trail a short distance and then drove the wagon down the road and directly into the river, just enough for the wagon wheels to go into the water, then turned the wagon downstream to make it look like the current had swept it away.

After dumping the wagon, the draft horses were driven a bit further down the river and lead out on a rocky beach, of sorts, so they wouldn't be easy to trace.

Since there were no other horses for them to ride, Clay, Jake and Julio each had to ride a draft horse. There were no saddles, which Jake complained about, but not Clay or Julio, because both of them knew the broad backs of a draft horse made it feel as comfortable as sitting on a saddle.

Clay was surprised when they headed south, instead of north and he said so. "You sure you're headed the right direction? Wichita is to the north."

Aaron Hammershield grinned and looked over at Clay, who was riding on the left side of him. "Yes, yes, it is. But I've decided we are not going that direction first. Wichita is a long ride from here and I do not envision such a trip on horseback. We will go down this side of the river until we find a safe place to cross, then turn east and head for Houston. There, I will sell the horses and tack and purchase train fare to Wichita."

Once again, Clay was reminded that he was not dealing with an ordinary outlaw.

"And I can assume you are planning to be reimbursed for your expenses on top of the reward?" Clay asked.

"You are very astute, my friend - very astute indeed – and speak well when it suits you. I wasn't aware they had schools in Kansas that taught that type of thinking; I thought that was done only back east."

Clay decided to not delve into his schooling, which didn't amount to much in the first place, he only went to the sixth grade. But his father was a well-traveled man and captain of a world-class schooner and his mother was an ex-schoolteacher. What he learned about life and sizin' up folks, along with readin', writin', ciferin' and such, he learned from the both of them. "There's a lot to be learned about people and life in general, that don't come from books. Although, readin' a lot sets the mind ta thinkin' about things, and ah thinkin' man can be ah strong adversary."

Hammershield looked at Clay and thought, 'this man is like a man with two faces. One side is a cowboy, and the other a scholar. This could prove to be very interesting.'

When Hammershield didn't respond, Clay continued. "You take that president that got his-self killed by that Ford fella, that Abraham Lincoln. He was president of these here United States and I hear tell he did a lot of good for this country, but I don't recall hearin' of him goin' ta college. The way I understand it, he was raised in Kentucky and Indiana by uneducated parents who moved around ah lot, and from what I heard or read, someplace, is what he learned come from five different schoolmasters, and the rest from lookin' around at what was goin' on, and then thinkin' on it.

"They musta been some good teachers and he musta listened right hard, cause he turned out ta be ah well-remembered man," Clay said with a broad grin.

After a moment, Hammershield spurred his mount and rode up ahead to be alone with his thoughts. He suddenly realized that Clay Brentwood was playing with him and knew he would have to be careful. He would have to watch this man's every move. The man would be looking for any opportunity he could find to escape, and he must not provide one. Hammershield felt an excitement surge through him – finally, here was someone he could match wits with, someone on his level. Harvard University, where he'd taught philosophy, was a long way from here and it had been some time since he'd matched wits with an educated man.

Jake rode up next to Clay and asked, "What did you say to him to make him ride off like that?"

"Nuthin' much," Clay said. "We was just talkin' about President Lincoln and all of ah sudden, he spurred his horse and rode off."

"President Lincoln? Why was you talkin' about…. never mind. You just watch what you say to The Hammer. He's ah short tempered man and I don't want him killing you before we get that money."

Clay grinned and said, "Nor do I," wondering when his chance to escape would come.

By mid-morning of the second day, south of where the massacre had occurred, the river had finally gone down and near a narrow part of the river they found a place to cross.

Once they were on the east side of the Brazos River, everyone seemed to be more relaxed. Clay rode up alongside Hammershield and asked, "How much further is it ta Houston?"

"We should be there in time to enjoy a decent evening meal," he said. "Why do you ask?"

"Ahh, no reason. Just wondering," Clay said, turning his horse to the side and dropping back a ways.

"Okay, Mister Brentwood, what kind of trick have you got up your sleeve now?" Hammershield said as he watched Clay ride away.

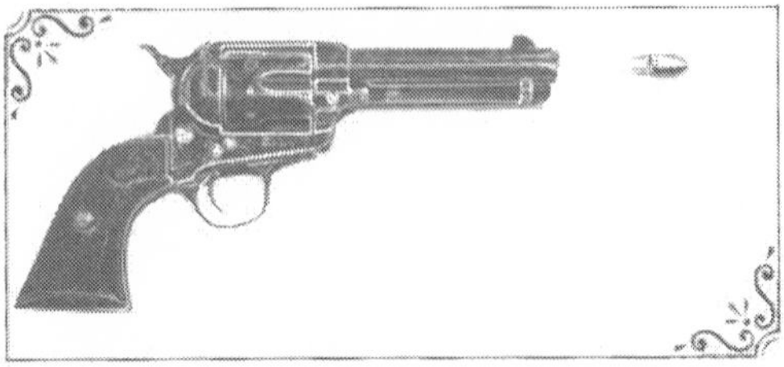

# CHAPTER FIFTEEN

Howard Loring and Bill McDaniel stood in the shadows of an alley across from Abigail Schuster's house and waited. Bill's legs were beginning to ache. He wasn't used to standing for long periods of time. "What time is it?" he whispered.

Howard reached into his vest pocket and retrieved a round, silver plated pocket watch and clicked open the cover. Holding it up toward the moonlight so he could see the dial, he said, "Seventeen minutes past midnight. He should be coming out soon."

He'd hardly gotten the words out when McDaniel said, "I think I see him coming now."

They pulled sacks over their heads that had holes in the front so they could see. When the judge was abreast of the alley, Bill

McDaniel stepped up behind him and grabbed him by the neck and hauled him into the darkness of the alley.

Howard Loring immediately placed his hand over the judge's mouth to keep him from yelling and in a deep-throated voice to disguise his own voice, said, "Be quiet and listen and maybe you'll live to see another day."

Judge Tyson was so scared he almost soiled himself, and stood still, waiting to see what was going to happen. He'd never been robbed before and wasn't sure what to do.

The deep-throated voice said, "Get out of town. Nobody wants you here. Leave and don't come back or you'll find yourself and your whore dangling from a tree limb."

The judge was shocked and tried to struggle, but Bill McDaniel had him in a neck hold that didn't allow for much movement without being strangled. This wasn't about being robbed. Someone was trying to run him out of town. He tried to see the man who was doing the talking but it was far too dark and he looked to be wearing a mask of some kind.

"I want you to understand the consequences of your staying here," the rough voice said. "The Austin Christian Committee has taken a vote and if you value your life, you and that jaded woman will leave on the next train. Your kind will not be allowed in Austin. Do I make myself clear?"

Judge Tyson was trying to make sense of what the man said. Would they really hang a woman? What kind of Christians would do such a thing? He shook his head 'yes,' as best he could, trying not to strangle himself.

Realizing they weren't going to kill him here in this alleyway, allowed his fear to subside somewhat. He was about to try to say something when he felt a sharp pain on the top of his head and everything went black.

When he opened his eyes, someone was shaking his shoulder and asking, "Hey mister, are you alright?"

The judge looked up into the face of a young boy of around ten or eleven. The boy helped him to his feet and he said, "Yes, I think so. I must have tripped and bumped my head, that's all. Thank you for your concern."

As the boy ran off down the sidewalk, the judge leaned against the side of the building, wondering how long he'd been lying here. It was daylight so it had to have been at least six hours. People were already walking up and down the sidewalks, doing their early morning shopping.

His head hurt something awful as he limped back across the street and knocked on the front door of Abigail's house.

When Abigail opened the door and saw the judge standing there with a trickle of blood running down his face, she fainted.

The judge shook her and when she opened her eyes, he helped her to her feet and stepped inside. As he turned to close the door, he saw two women standing in front of the house, staring at him. He slammed the door and cursed. "Damn them. Damn them to hell."

The judge's swearing confused Abigail, who was just recovering from seeing the blood on Horatio's face. He'd never cursed in front of her before.

"My poor Horatio, what has happened to you? Who did this and why are you cursing all of a sudden?"

Easing himself onto a kitchen chair, he explained what had happened while Abigail cleaned the blood from his face and out of his hair, and then put some ointment on his head that stung like all get-out.

When she'd finished, she poured each of them a cup of coffee, laced with just a wee bit of whiskey, "for medicinal purposes," she said.

"I've never heard of an Austin Christian Committee. Are you sure that's what he said?"

"Of course, I'm sure. Do you think I'm deaf?"

"Oh, I didn't mean…"

"Never mind what you meant," Horatio snarled. "It's probably some new group somebody dreamed up, just to raise a fuss," the judge said as he took a long drink of the whiskey laced coffee and sighed.

"What are we going to do?" Abigail asked. "I can't just up and leave my home! And I'm sure I wouldn't be able to sell it in one day! Oh Horatio, what are we going to do?"

Horatio held out his cup and she filled it with more of the whiskey-laced coffee. The judge took a sip and felt the pain in his head easing somewhat. "Yes, you do have a dilemma, don't you?"

Horatio Tyson's mind was running at high speed, trying to come up with a plan and after a long moment, he said, "Here's what we'll do. First, I don't believe they would do harm to a woman, especially such a fine, upstanding woman such as yourself. So, you could stay here long enough to get the house sold, which I would guess to be no more than a few days; this being such a very fine house."

But what about you, Horatio, what will you do? Didn't they say they would hang you if you stayed here?"

Horatio took another sip of coffee and felt the harshness of the whiskey warming his insides.

"Yes, that's exactly what they said, and I believe they meant it, which means I cannot stay here. I must leave, immediately."

Horatio reached up and pulled Abigail down onto his lap and kissed her on the neck, and said, "But I can't stand us being apart."

"Oh, but if you stay here, they'll hang you!" Abigail gasped.

"Well…" Horatio said, "I guess we have only one real option. I'll leave today and go to a prearranged place, say, Denver, and you can meet me there as soon as you get the house sold."

Abigail sighed. "Yes, I guess that's the only sensible option."

"Good," Horatio said, pushing her off his lap and standing up. "The sooner the better, I think."

Taking her by the shoulders, he leaned in and kissed her passionately, then said, "While I'm packing, why don't you go down to the train depot and buy our tickets. I'll meet you there shortly. That way I can be out of town before they know I'm gone and you can see someone about selling your house. The quicker you get this place sold, the quicker we can be together, again."

Abigail smiled grudgingly, seeing the logic in his words. "Alright," she said as she picked up her purse.

When she'd gone, Horatio went into her bedroom and took the decorative, flower covered jar that held Abigail's life's savings down from the shelf and counted out a thousand dollars. He put the money in his pocket and put what was left, back into the container. After all, he didn't want to leave her destitute, he only wanted a little traveling money, which he felt she owed him for all the favors he'd done for her. Besides, she would have the money from selling her house to add to what was left in the container.

Back in his apartment, Horatio hurriedly packed two bags; one with a few law books and the other with the few clothes he had. Once he got to Denver, he could decide where he would go from there. For a few dollars, he could get a fake law degree to match the new name he would create for himself. He would start over, somewhere, like California or maybe go up to Canada. No one would find him there. And like the other women he'd left behind, Abigail would pine for a little while, and then she would get over him. But he would definitely not be in Denver when she arrived, if she ever did. It might take her months.

Howard Loring and Bill McDaniel were almost to the point of rolling on the floor with laughter as they watched through Bill's office window as Horatio Tyson hustled down the sidewalk in the direction of the train station, a suitcase in each hand, just as the train was pulling in.

"I… I can't believe it would be so easy, or that he would be so gullible," Howard said between gasping for air.

"For a judge, he sure ain't very bright," Bill said, flopping down into his office chair and opening the top, left hand drawer with one hand while wiping the tears from his eyes with the other.

Pulling out a bottle of Rye whiskey, he said, "I do believe we deserve a reward for pulling off stage one of your brilliant plan, Mister Attorney at Law."

When they heard the train whistle stating it was leaving the station, Howard lifted his cup and said, "Ah, the wicked web we weave when trying to deceive."

"And victory is bittersweet." the ranger announced, raising his cup to his lips.

When the train could no longer be heard and they saw Abigail Schuster passing the window, headed in the direction of her house, Howard said, “Let us not congratulate ourselves too quickly. We still have stage two before we can have any room to breathe.

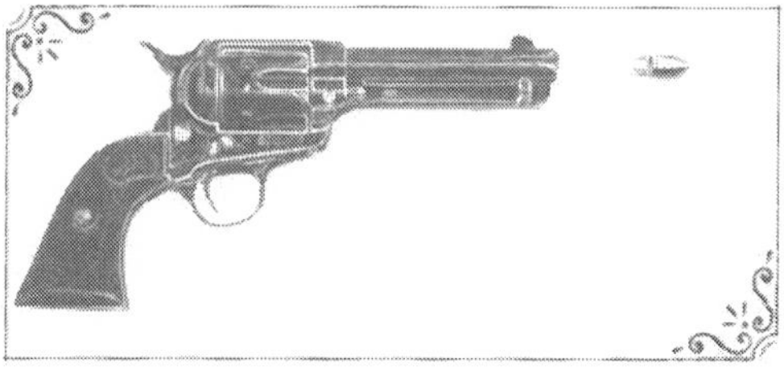

# CHAPTER SIXTEEN

-

Houston loomed in the near distance around what Clay figured to be somewhere close to five o'clock in the afternoon. He didn't know for sure because Hammershield had taken his watch from Bull, the guard, who had taken it from him. When he'd asked for it back, the answer had been, "In good time, my friend, in good time."

At the edge of town, Hammershield pulled them to a halt and drew his pistol and pointed it at the three prisoners as he reached inside his coat pocket and pulled out a sheriff's badge. "I picked this up from a sheriff up in Arkansas who doesn't need it anymore," he said, chuckling to himself.

Then, without a word, he shot Jake Comers in the left eye, and then turned the pistol on Julio and shot him in the chest. Both men were knocked out of the saddle --- dead by the time they hit the ground.

"Put them over their saddles," he said. Four men dismounted and did his bidding. As they went about doing as they were told, Hammershield looked at Clay, who sat on the draft horse, his face showing no emotion. "One prisoner is easier to watch than three," Hammershield said nonchalantly. "Plus, now I only have to take these two as far as Houston. And I like the fact that there will be two less to split with."

Clay stared at Hammershield's eyes and felt a cold chill run down his spine. The man was just like Curly Beeler, a cold-blooded killer. How he would get away before they got to Wichita, he didn't know, but he would keep his eyes open for an opportunity, knowing he would have to be careful. Even though the man wanted money from him, if he felt threatened, he would shoot him just as quick as he did Jake and Julio. He felt sorry for Julio. He felt, given the chance, Julio would have gone straight.

When they got into Houston, they went straight to the City Marshal's office and Aaron Hammershield presented himself as a sheriff from Arkansas and told him he was taking a prisoner back to Wichita to stand trial for murder.

The marshal, a sad looking example of a lawman, with his fat, round, sad eyed face and rotund stomach, dressed in an ill-fitting suit and dirty white shirt that had food stains all down the front, told Hammershield his name was Ryan Sugarbaker.

Hammershield motioned for the marshal to follow him and took him out into the street, where he showed him the bodies of Jake and Julio. He told the marshal he had been transporting them back to Arkansas to stand trial for rustling cattle and horses, but shortly after crossing the Brazos, they had tried to escape and his deputies had to shoot them. He told the marshal he wanted to bury them here in Houston and wondered if, for a small price, the marshal would mind signing an affidavit as a witness to the burials.

The marshal viewed the bodies and nodded his head in agreement. They were dead and that was a fact and he could collect ten dollars just for signing his name.

The marshal also agreed to keep Clay in jail while Hammershield arranged for train passage to Wichita. Hammershield informed the marshal of the kind of man he was holding. "He's slick tongued and will tell you lies with a straight face and then put a knife in your back. He's a cold-blooded killer without a conscience. He went on a shooting spree down in New

Mexico and killed twelve law abiding citizens without so much as a, by your leave. Be careful and watch him like a hawk. I'll put one of my deputies here with you through the night to make sure he doesn't pull a fast one."

The marshal looked at Clay and shook his head, convinced he had a real bad hombre in his jail, and sighed, happy for the help. He hated violence, but he did like the power and respect that came with being city marshal.

They brought Clay his supper, which consisted of a small steak, beans, tortillas and a cup of coffee. They gave him only a spoon to eat with, so he had to pick up the meat with his hand and bite off chunks.

Clay toyed with his food, his mind reliving the years since Martha had died, and wondered what was going to happen next. Did he really deserve to be hung for what he'd done? He had, in fact, willfully ridden into Bristol Springs, intent on bringing justice to Curly and his gang. Was that cold bloodied murder? At the time he'd leaned on what the good book said, 'an eye for an eye,' but lookin' back, he wasn't so sure.

And did those men who kidnapped the women with the intent to sell them into slavery, deserve to be executed in front of a firing squad?

How many men's death had he caused during the past four years? As best as he could figure, it was in the neighborhood of thirty.

But they were bad men, he kept telling himself. Men who were a menace to the human race - men who would continue to bring harm and sorrow wherever they went.

But, he was not a lawman, nor was he a judge or jury. So how did he think he had the right or the power to sit in judgment over them?

He'd never wanted any of this, but it had come his way and he'd done what his conscience told him to do. And for that, he was considered a murderer, at least by Judge Tyson.

As he lay on his bunk staring at the ceiling, he knew he had to figure a way to redeem himself in the eyes of the law and go back to his ranch where he could settle down and forget the past.

It was long after midnight before Clay finally drifted off to sleep.

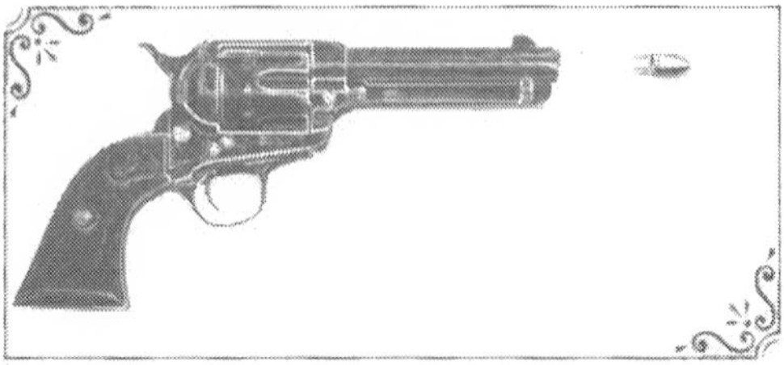

# CHAPTER SEVENTEEN

-

Howard Loring followed Bill McDaniel up the steps of the governor's mansion just as the governor was about to enter.

"Governor, I have something very important to talk to you about," Bill McDaniel said, following him inside.

The governor turned and was about to make a reply when he spotted Howard Loring, and changed what he was about to say, in mid-sentence.

"Mister McDaniel, what.... what's he doing here? He's not..."

"Whoa. Hold on governor," Bill said, raising his hands, palms forward. "I think when you hear what I have to say, you just may change your mind about the judge and Clay Brentwood, the man he sentenced to hang at Huntsville prison."

Once again, the governor tried to object, but with Bill on one arm and Howard on the other, they marched him to his office and deposited him in his chair behind his desk.

The judge looked at them wide eyed and a bit intimidated. Bill McDaniel had not become head of the Texas Rangers without gaining a certain reputation.

After Bill closed and locked the office door so they wouldn't be interrupted, he walked over and stood next to Howard in front of the governor's desk.

"Now, Sir, I'm going to tell you a story and then I'll let Mister Loring finish it, and when we're finished, I believe you'll believe as we do, that Judge Horatio Tyson was acting under the influence of Miss Abigail Schuster and was given an unjust sentence."

The governor turned his head and looked out of his window. The sun was shining brightly and suddenly a calm came over him that he hadn't experienced in some time. Turning back, he said, "You're sure he's gone? Judge Tyson, I mean."

Bill McDaniel nodded his head. "Yes sir. He left on the morning train for Denver, and before he left, he stole a thousand dollars from Miss Schuster. That's the kind of upstanding man you've been dealing with. And I'm sure she gave him a lot more money that she isn't complaining about."

The governor shook his head; relieved that, that low-life creature who had lately made his life a living hell would no longer be blackmailing him. Looking up at the two men in front of his desk, he said, "I agree that we need to do something about Mister Brentwood, but what can I do? He's already been sent to Huntsville."

Bill laid both of his hands on the governor's desk and leaned toward him. "Glad you asked, governor. Mister Loring and I," he said, nodding his head in Howard's direction, "have been discussing that very topic, and I think we've come up with a solution that will not only satisfy you, but also allow Mister Brentwood to be punished for what he did, but in a more civilized way."

"You have my attention, Mister McDaniel."

"Well sir, first, you will need to telegraph the warden at Huntsville and rescind the order to hang Mister Brentwood."

"Yes, Mister McDaniel, I think that is a very good idea. Then what?"

Bill grinned and straightened up and looked at Howard, who explained his idea to the governor and watched as the governor's eyes lit up.

By his expression, they felt the governor bought it. Now, all they had to do was make it official. There was no way he could say no. This idea would put him in good standing with the people and if he decided to retire, he would go out as the most progressive governor to ever hold office in the state of Texas.

The governor smiled and said, "I think that's a very good idea, gentlemen. Yes, a very good idea. It's a new way to deal with criminals."

Howard Loring said, "If I may be so bold. When the public finds out, we say this was your idea. That way you can retire with dignity and in good standing with the people of Texas for being such a liberal thinker."

Two hours later, a telegram came back from the Huntsville warden, stating the prison wagon had not showed up and he had no idea where it might be.

Bill swore under his breath. "Damn."

"What's that, Mister McDaniel?" the governor asked.

"Nothing worth repeating," Bill said. "But if you could assign me to this case, I promise you I'll find the answer to their disappearance."

It didn't't' take the governor any more time than to write out the order. He wanted to be remembered as a governor the people respected.

As Bill and Howard walked back toward Bill's office, Howard said, "I'm coming with you, and I'll hear no argument."

To Howard's surprise, Bill nodded his head; "You'll get no argument from me. I can use the company. Besides, you've earned the right, and to keep it legal, I'll deputize you."

By noon, the two men were in the saddle, leading packhorses and headed east, following the same trail the prison wagon had taken. A hawk soared high above them in the warm afternoon sun, searching for its next meal.

By early afternoon on the second day, they reached the Brazos River. The tracks of the prison wagon had almost been blown away by the dry, Texas wind, but not quite. Here and there the deep tracks of the wagon could be seen, right up to the edge of the river where they disappeared.

There had been no more rain, so they were able to cross without any problems. On the opposite shore, they saw no evidence of the wagon leaving the river.

"From what I can see, it looks like they tried to cross the river and didn't make it," Howard said, searching the ground for tracks.

Bill McDaniel, a man with a suspicious mind, turned his horse and went back across the river. "Maybe. There was a rainstorm and the Brazos is known to flood and has claimed the lives of both man and animal, but my gut is tellin' me, that's not what happened."

Howard had a confused look on his face. "What are you saying? What else is there to…" and then it hit him. "You think there was foul play? Who and why?"

"I don't know," Bill said as he emerged onto the road again, and stepped down from the saddle, rubbing his back. "You watch the horses," he said, handing the reins of his horse to Howard. "I'm gonna scout around a little," he said as he took a pair of moccasins from his saddle bag and put them on. At Howard's questioning look, he said, "I don't want to mess up any evidence that might still be here."

He walked around the campsite, slowly, his eyes searching the ground. The first thing he found was, all evidence of anyone being here had been swept up. "Strange," he said to himself. There should have been tracks of some kind; some evidence of use, but there was nothing but a fire pit that had been used not long ago.

Next, he moved into the wooded area and hadn't gone far when his eyes noticed a dark spot on some leaves. He stooped down, brushing away leaves that had blown over the spot. Blood, it was definitely blood, but human or animal, he couldn't tell.

Standing up, he ventured deeper into the trees, his eyes searching for anything out of place, and after only a short distance, he saw where several horses had stood, bunched up.

Turning, he walked back and swung into the saddle, telling Howard what he'd found. They rode north along the river, searching for more tracks, but after a mile, they found none and turned back. By then, it was coming onto late evening and Bill knew it would be dark soon. He decided they should spend the night at the campsite and head south along the river in the morning.

Howard was amazed at how quickly the evidence had changed from accidental death to the possibility of… he didn't know what, but from what Bill said, there had been several men waiting in the trees. The leaves with the blood on them was still a mystery. It looked as though someone had been injured, but who; they had no idea. And unless they were up to no good, why had they tried to hide their being there?

The next morning after a quick breakfast of bacon and coffee, they mounted up and rode south along the river, scouting for tracks.

A day and a half later, a little before midday, Howard saw their sign and reined up.

"Over here," he shouted.

Bill McDaniel had been searching a little farther from the water, giving them a wider area of search. He turned his horse and rode up alongside Howard and looked to where he was pointing.

"Yup. Looks like we've found them, and they crossed the river right here."

"Wonder why they came so far south before crossing?" Howard said, looking over at Bill.

"More than likely, two reasons," Bill said. First, they had to wait for the river to go down and they needed to be away from that campsite. And second, I figure they're headed for Houston, which is pretty much, due east of here."

"Houston… Why would they want to go to Houston?"

Bill studied the far side of the river for a moment, then said, "Now that's ah right good question, and I reckon the only way we'll find the answer to that is for us to go to Houston." And with that, he touched his boots to the sides of his horse and headed for the eastern shore of the river.

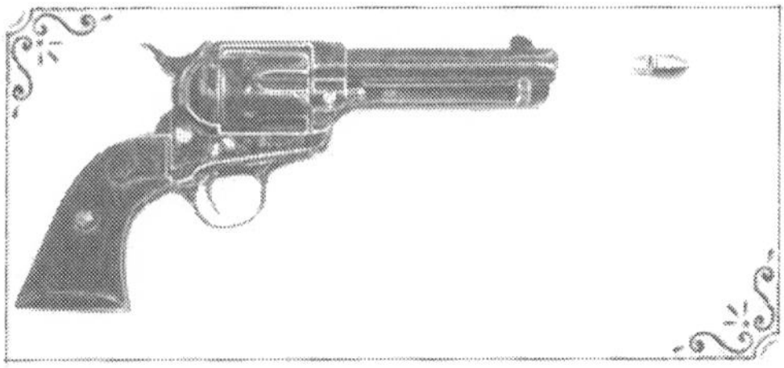

# CHAPTER EIGHTEEN

At six o'clock the next afternoon they boarded the train and once again, Clay was back in handcuffs and leg irons. Hammershield told him it was just for appearances. After all, he was supposed to be a sheriff taking his prisoner back to stand trial and this is what people expected to see, no offense intended.

Clay's gut told him the man was lying. He stared out of the window, watching the passing landscape, which amounted to just more of the same thing. Texas was, for the most part, miles and miles of nothing but miles and miles. Over and over, his mind kept asking the same question, "How am I gonna get outta this mess?"

Getting away from Hammershield and his men was the first problem. Next would be figuring out how to get his sentence rescinded and become a free man, again – if something like that was even possible.

He looked around the train car and saw nothing of Hammershield. He was more than likely in the lounge car, drinking and telling some made-up story about what he went through to capture Clay and the other two, who had tried to escape and wound up getting themselves killed – assuring them he had Clay well-guarded.

Clay chuckled to himself as he looked around and saw at least four of the guards setting in places where they could watch him at all times. They were probably doing it in shifts. Hammershield was playing his role to the fullest, expecting to get his money back and more.

Trying to attract one of the guard's attention, he said, "Excuse me, but can I get something to read? A book, a newspaper, anything."

Not one of them paid him the slightest attention, then out of nowhere a young woman came down the aisle and sat down beside him, handing him a folded newspaper. "I don't have a book, but this is the latest edition of the Houston Star. There's even a story about you, right on the front page, Mister Brentwood," she said with a big smile.

Clay looked at her and noticed she was wearing a white dress with red roses on the shoulders. Her soft brown hair hung down around her shoulders, flowing from under a large, wide brimmed sun hat. She had large brown eyes, a wide smile that would melt butter, and a complexion that said she spent a lot of time outside, nicely tanned but not burnt.

Before he could say anything, one of the guards grabbed the young lady by the arm and pulled her to a standing position. "You can't sit there. He's a criminal and ain't allowed ta have nobody sittin' with him, so you just go on back to your own seat. Now git..." he said, giving her a shove back down the aisle.

"All I did was give him a newspaper to read," she said, indignantly, sticking her tongue out at him, then turned and walked out of the car and into the next one.

"And you keep your trap shut," the guard said to Clay before he turned and went back to his seat.

Clay said nothing but turned his attention to the newspaper and the weight he felt in his lap. He laid his hand on the paper and felt the shape of a pistol in between the pages. Casually, he looked around to see how close the guards were watching him, and when he saw they weren't paying much attention, he picked up the paper and opened it, allowing the pistol to lay on his lap, hidden behind the newspaper.

Glancing down, he saw a fairly new, forty-four Colt repeating pistol. With one hand hidden behind the newspaper, he slowly slid the pistol from his lap to the side of his left leg, which was next to the window and couldn't be seen by anyone.

Who was that young lady? And what prompted her to do such a thing? She had taken a big chance. His brain was reeling, trying to put a name to her face, but for the life of him, nothing came to mind.

"Okay, Brentwood, on your feet. Suppertime," one of the guards, a short stump of a man in rumpled clothes, said, looking down at him.

Clay jumped and almost panicked until his mind registered the man was only telling him it was suppertime.

"Sure," he said, laying the paper on top of the pistol and scooting it next to the edge of the seat cushion, then pressing his hand down, he shoved the pistol in between the seat and the wall of the train. With the paper lying over it, it couldn't be seen. He would figure out what to do with it when he came back from eating.

Giving a sigh, he stood up and made his way to the aisle, then shuffled off in the direction of the dining car.

He had a small steak, vegetables and coffee for his evening meal. It was waiting for him when he slid into the booth. The guards sat in the booth across the aisle from him and had their supper at the same time. He tried to ask a few questions of them, such as how much longer to Wichita, and other questions that really meant very little. All of his questions were ignored without so much as a glance his way. Finally, he gave up and turned his mind to the pistol, while he ate.

How was he going to conceal it when he went to bed? Would he be sleeping in a Pullman or would he be expected to sleep in his seat? Sticking it in his waistband was not an option, either.

After supper, they took him back to his seat and found the young lady sitting there looking pretty as a picture.

"Hey, get outta there! I done told you, he ain't allowed ta have nobody sittin' with him. Now go on back ta wherever you come from," the guard yelled.

"Oh pooh, you're just no fun at all. I just wanted to talk to him. He's a famous man, you know. I read all about him in the newspaper."

"Don't make no difference. You can't sit there! Now git; or do I half'ta call the sheriff?"

"Oh, all right. I'm going. But I still think you're an ole stuck in the mud."

And with that, she huffed down the aisle, her skirts making a swishing noise.

Clay grinned as he watched her go, then looked at the guard who shook his head and went over to his seat and sat down, glaring at Clay.

Clay waited a few minutes before he laid his hand on the newspaper and with relief, felt the pistol, still in its hiding place. When he picked up the newspaper, a note fell out and dropped onto his lap.

Behind the concealment of the newspaper, Clay opened the piece of paper and looked at it. It was in a nicely written hand, in ink, on a piece of paper that made him want to sneeze. He wasn't used to paper that had perfume on it.

Once again, checking to see that he wasn't being watched too closely, he moved his eyes slightly, checking the guards with his peripheral vision. None of them seemed to be paying him any attention, so he took a chance and read the note.

Dear Mister Brentwood, we know about your situation. We are your friends and want to help… There will be an incident before we get to Fort Worth. Be ready.

Clay read it twice, still confused. She'd used the word, we, instead of, I. Who were these, we, she mentioned? And how far were they from Fort Worth? How much time did he have before the incident - whatever that was supposed to mean? Well, whatever was going to happen, he'd better be ready. He raised the note and stuck it in his mouth and began to chew.

"Hey," the guard sitting across the aisle from him, yelled. "What're you eatin'?"

Clay swallowed and wished he had some coffee or water to help wash the paper down.

"Just ah piece of biscuit I brought back with me from supper," Clay said with a grin.

"I don't believe you," the man said as he stood up and leaned in and grabbed Clay's jaw. "Open up!"

Clay opened his mouth and said, "Ahh. Do my tonsils look okay?"

The guard released his jaw and stepped back. "Don't you be eatin' nuthin' less'un you get permission; you hear what I'm sayin'?"

"Yes sir," Clay said as he brought his cuffed hands up in a mock salute.

"You just mind your smart mouth, mister. The boss never said we couldn't rough you up ah bit, and that would suit me just fine."

"Yeah, you boys are real tough, as long as I'm shackled and handcuffed, but how would you stand up in a bare fisted, knock-down-drag-out?" Clay asked.

And for that remark, he got a backhand slap across his face. "Just maybe we'll get ta find out before this is all over," the guard said as he stood up and glared down at Clay.

Clay turned his head and looked out of the window. He didn't need to get his face battered up - at least not when he couldn't do anything about it.

The guard reached down and grabbed Clay's newspaper and took it with him back to his seat.

Clay scooted closer to the window, hiding the pistol with his leg. He hadn't been sitting there long, when the conductor came down the aisle and when he was close, he called out, "Fort Worth within the hour. Fort Worth within the hour." And when he passed Clay, he looked down and winked.

Clay made a slight nod, thinking he looked young for a conductor. The conductor grinned and went on down the aisle.

So, the conductor was in on whatever was gonna happen and he'd been given a warning to get ready. Well, he thought to himself, there wasn't much he could do except wait until the action started, then grab the pistol and play it by ear.

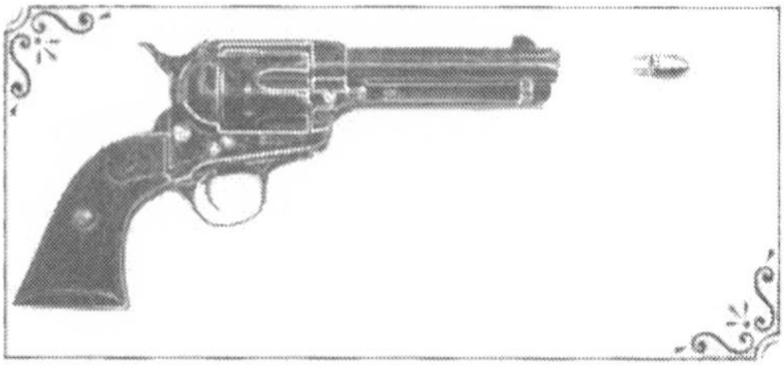

# CHAPTER NINETEEN

As soon as Bill McDaniel and Howard Loring got into Houston, they went straight to the local sheriff's office and reported in – told him their story, and to their surprise, found out what had happened to Clay at the hands of the supposed sheriff from Arkansas.

Bill McDaniel walked over and without asking, poured a cup of coffee and blew on it to cool it off before taking a sip. Howard Loring and Marshal Sugarbaker stood watching the famous ranger as he thought over the situation.

"Think I need to mosey over to the telegraph office and send out ah wire to ah friend of mine in Little Rock," Bill said as he sat the cup of unfinished coffee on the marshal's desk.

"I see there's a restaurant across the street. How's the food?" Bill asked.

"Well, I think it's very good. I eat there all the time," the marshal said.

"In that case, I'll meet the two of you over there for lunch as soon as I'm finished down at the telegraph office," Bill said as he headed for the door. Just before he left the marshal's office, he looked over his shoulder, eyed the marshal and said, "If you're any example, I'm sure the food is excellent."

Howard hid a grin as he watched the overweight marshal grin from ear to ear, never realizing he'd just been ribbed.

Howard and the marshal were enjoying a cup of coffee when Bill came in and walked over and sat down at their table.

"Kinda like I figured," he said. "My friend in Little Rock said Aaron Hammershield has paper on him for murder, extortion, and a number of other things. He also said there is evidence that Hammershield killed the sheriff up in Arkansas and took his money, his badge, holster and handgun."

"I don't understand," the marshal said in a conversational manner, looking at the other patrons who recognized the famous ranger. The stories he would tell later about working with the head of the Texas Rangers.

Howard Loring jumped into the conversation, addressing his words to Bill. “Correct me if I’m wrong, Bill, but it seems to me, this Hammershield somehow found out that Clay Brentwood has money in the bank up in Wichita and by springing him from the prison wagon, he figures Clay will think he owes him a reward; but to keep Clay under his control until he gets the money, he’s holding Clay under lock and key and pretending to be a sheriff from Arkansas, transporting a prisoner.”

“That’s about the way I have it figured, too,” Bill said, signaling for the waitress.

Ryan Sugarbaker’s jaw was hanging open in amazement. “I guess he made a damn fool out of me,” he said, shaking his head.

“Don’t be so hard on yourself, marshal. You had no way of knowing,” Bill said as the waitress came up to the table.

“The usual?” she asked of the marshal, who shook his head yes.

Later, when they were back at the marshal’s office, Bill patted his stomach and said, “You were right, they do serve good food, especially that pecan pie.”

The marshal beamed, and then plopped down in his chair and asked, “So, what are you going to do now?”

“How much of a head start do they have?” Bill asked.

"Let's see, they left around six yesterday evening, and it's one pm now…"

"Nineteen hours," Howard said.

"When does the next train leave going north?" Bill asked.

"Not for another two days," Marshal Sugarbaker said, shrugging his shoulders.

Bill McDaniel was looking out the window of the marshal's office, watching people go up and down the sidewalk when he heard a train whistle. "What's that?" he asked.

"Oh, that's just the spare engine we keep down at the train yard to move cars around," Sugarbaker said.

"That's it!" Bill said as he grabbed his hat from the hat rack just inside the door. "Com'on."

"What's it?" Howard said, rushing to catch up with Bill McDaniel.

As they hurried down the street, walking much faster than Ryan Sugarbaker wanted to go, he yelled at the fast walking ranger's back. "What are you planning to do?"

"To catch up with them, if we can," Bill called over his shoulder.

At this point, even Howard was confused, but kept his mouth shut. He didn't want to sound like an idiot, asking stupid questions.

Once they got to the train yard, Bill wasted no time and went straight to the engine and climbed aboard.

"Hey, you can't be in here. Now get off before I call the marshal," the engineer yelled over the sound of the engine.

Bill McDaniel pulled open his jacket and revealed the Texas Ranger badge pinned to his vest. "No need to. He's standing just over yonder," he said, pointing to where Howard and the marshal were standing.

"Okay, Ranger," the engineer, a large man with a mat of reddish gray hair and a long, bushy mustache that showed signs of chewing tobacco stains on it. The people of Houston knew him only as, O'Brien. "And just what might ah Texas Ranger be wantin' with me engine?"

"I'm commandeering it and you in the name of the Texas Rangers. You'll only be hauling three cars; one loaded with wood, a boxcar for the horses and a caboose for us to ride in. You'll be paid for your time, of course."

The big Irishman grinned. He'd always dreamed that one day he would get to see what this engine would actually do. So far, he'd only been allowed to get her up to twenty-five miles an hour, but he was sure she would go much faster. "Sounds like ya need ta get somewhere in ah hurry."

"I do," Bill said, letting the flap of his jacket fall back down, hiding the badge. "We need to do some hi-balling. I'm chasing the train that left here last night at six."

O'Brien, whistled. "That's ah tall order, me bucko, but with all the stops she has between here and Fort Worth, if I push her to the limit, we just might be able ta do it. I'll be ah needin' ah stoker, though."

From the ground, just outside the engine, Howard called up, "I'll help pay," he said, knowing Clay wouldn't mind him using some of the money he'd left with him.

Forty-five minutes later, the small train pulling only three cars was headed north with the engineer yelling, "More wood. Let's see what this ole darlin' can really do!"

Inside the caboose, Bill McDaniel was pacing back and forth. At the back door, he looked out of the small window and saw the landscape disappearing faster than it usually did, and he smiled. The big Irishman was being true to his word. He was trying to set a new speed record and doing a good job.

"Think the horses will be alright?" Howard asked.

"I think so," Bill answered, nodding his head. "They can't move around much in the stalls. They should be just fine."

Ryan Sugarbaker could hardly stand it. His stomach was doing flip-flops. He was actually chasing criminals, alongside the famous Texas Ranger, Big Bill McDaniel. This story would get him free drinks at the saloon for years to come. Maybe he would write a book about this adventure! If he played his cards right, he might become famous.

Howard looked out of the side window, then turned to Bill. "How fast do you think we're going?"

"Not sure, but it's faster than I've ever been on a train. Maybe, I'll just go up and see," Bill said, heading for the door.

Making his way up on top of the boxcar and then trying to walk across the length without losing his hat or balance was a chore, and when he finally jumped onto the car hauling the wood, he saw that a lot had already been used.

When he climbed down and got into the engine compartment, he found the big Irishman, grinning from ear to ear.

"Looks like we're making good time," Bill yelled over the noise.

"Forty-two miles an hour and gainin'," the engineer yelled back. "If we can hold this speed straight through, we just might catch up with that train yer ah chasin'."

Bill reached into his jacket pocket and pulled out a pint bottle of whiskey and held it out in the engineer's direction. "I'm sure working this hard makes a man ah mite thirsty and I figured you'd like this better than water."

O'Brien wiped the back of his hand across his mouth, then reached for the bottle of whiskey. "It's thankin' ya kindly, I am. Yes, this will hit the spot."

When O'Brien handed the bottle back to Bill, it was half empty. He smiled as he handed the bottle to the stoker, who took a long pull before handing the bottle back to Bill, just as O'Brien yelled, "More wood!"

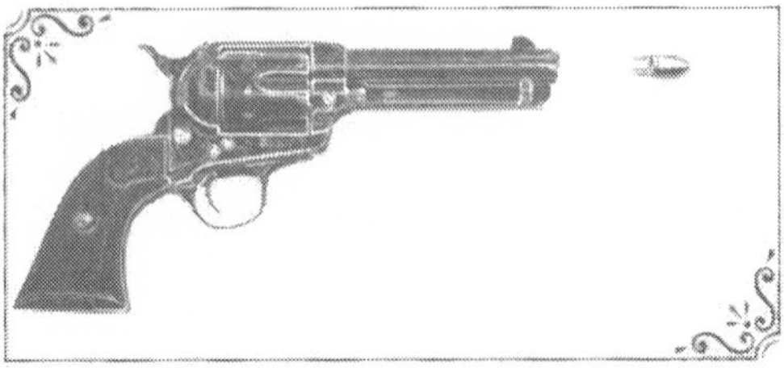

# CHAPTER TWENTY

-

It was barely ten minutes after the conductor had come through, announcing the arrival time into Fort Worth, when the train began to slow down and the rear door of the car came crashing open and Aaron Hammershield came stumbling into the car, his hands tied behind his back and a rope around his neck. Just behind Hammershield was the young conductor, holding the end of the rope in one hand and a pistol in the other.

At the noise, the guards started to rise. Clay pulled the pistol up and pointed it at them and yelled, "Hold it right there!"

The young girl and another man came in the opposite door. The girl had a pistol in her hand and the other man, dressed in overalls, and wearing a wide brimmed work hat, who looked like he might be her father, was holding a shotgun.

The older man said, in a very level voice, "If you want to see another day, drop your weapons onto the seat and raise your hands in the air. Anybody who wants to give me an excuse to pull the trigger on this here scatter gun, just have at it."

The guards looked at their leader, then as one, gently pulled their pistols from the holsters and dropped them onto the seats, then raised their heads.

When that was done, they were all seated in different seats and tied up, the girl went through Hammershield's pockets until she found the key that would unlock Clay's restraints.

Twenty minutes from the time it started, it was over. They had stopped the train and the engineer was complaining loudly about keeping his schedule to a young man of about twenty, who just grinned and said the train could be on its way when his pa said it could, and in the meantime, they'd just wait.

Standin next to the door where they could keep an eye on the prisoners, Clay could finally ask the question that had been plaguing him. "Beggin' your pardon," he said, "but along with thanking you for pullin' my fat outta the fire, so ta speak, I'm wonderin' who you folks are and why did you do it?"

The older man, leaned back in his seat and said, "Well, it's kind of ah long story, but I'll try and say it with as few ah words as I can.

"Ya see, you didn't know it, but we'd been trailin' Curly Beeler and his gang, too. Like you, we was aimin' ta send him to his maker, but you beat us to the punch."

"I don't understand," Clay said.

"Name's Clem Anderson, and this here is my daughter, Emma. The one who is pertindin' ta be the conductor, is my son, Israel, and my other son, Samuel, is up there with the engineer. He's the one who stopped the train til we get this thing all figured out.

"We're from Arkansas. Curly Beeler and his bunch of thievin' no-goods come through our part of the country on one of their rampages, and ta make ah long story short, they raided our place while me and my two boys, was out tendin' our crops. They raped and killed my wife and while one off 'em was tryin't ta rape my daughter, here," he said pointing at the girl, she up an grabbed his pistol and shot him, then ran off inta the woods behind the house, and come lookin' fer me and her brothers."

Clay nodded his head. "I see. A very similar situation to mine; but how did you know I was on this train?"

"Now that was providence," Clem Anderson said with a grin. "We just happened ta be in Houston visitin' with my wife's sister, Claire, and her husband, Rory. He runs ah feed and seed store there. Needed to tell her about the death of her sister, Maude.

"I see and somehow you saw or heard about me?" Clay asked.

"That was right peculiar too. My son, Samuel, well, he was in town pickin' up ah few things and was walking down the sidewalk, when he saw you come ridin' down the street, all trussed up like some kind o' criminal. Well now, he just sorta sundered down the sidewalk and saw you bein' taken inta the sheriff's office.

"Then over to the saloon, he heard the sheriff ah braggin' bout havin' this here murderer in his jail and about that sheriff who was takin' him up ta Wichita."

Well, how did you decide to come rescue me?" Clay asked.

"I'm comin' ta that," Clem said. "Well, like I said, Samuel was gatherin' information while nursin' a couple of beers, then come ah racin' back to Claire and Rory's place, wound up tighter than an eight-day clock. He said that Hammershield feller looked just like the one said to 'of shot sheriff Bigalow Bodine, who's ah second cousin of ours twice removed. So, we decided you was in trouble, and since it was you who'd helped us, so's ta say, with that Curly Beeler and his bunch, we decided ta return the favor."

Clay stood there looking at them, speechless.

"Maybe you'd like some air while we figure out what to do about this bunch," Emma said, taking his arm and heading for the door.

Clay noticed Mister Anderson and his son stayed on the train.

Outside, Clay noticed the sun had been replaced with a full moon and a sky filled with stars.

"Sure is ah purty night, don'tcha think?" Emma said, squeezing his arm.

"Yes, a very pretty night," he said, removing her hand and moving a short ways away.

"Mind if I smoke?" he asked, reaching for a cigarillo.

"Sure, it's ok," Emma said; her bottom lip curled up in a pout. "Pa and my brother Samuel, both smoke ah pipe, but not me or Israel: but ta be truthful, Israel does enjoy ah chew from time ta time."

About that time, to Clay's relief, Samuel and the engineer came hurrying down the side of the train.

When they got close, the engineer looked at Clay and asked, "You the one in charge?"

Clay scratched his nose and said, "Well, I…"

The engineer interrupted Clay and said, "See here young man, I have a schedule to keep and there are passengers who are wanting to know what's going on. What do I tell them and when can we leave?"

Clay looked up and could see faces of men, women and children pressed against the windows of the passenger cars. He looked from the engineer to the girl, and then to Samuel.

Samuel looked back at him and said, "I reckon it's up to you, Mister Brentwood. We come on this here train ta rescue you and now we have, so I reckon how you deal with'um is up ta you."

Clay looked up at the moon and wondered what he was supposed to do? If they went on into Fort Worth, how could he explain that he had been convicted of murder and sentenced to hang in Huntsville, but along the way, he'd been rescued by a crook named Hammershield, who killed the driver of the prison wagon as well as the two guards, who then held him prisoner until he could provide reward money, which is in a bank up in Wichita, and that's why they were travelin' on the train, which got taken over by the Anderson's in order to rescue him from

Hammershield, because of feelin' indebted to him for shootin' Curly Beeler and his gang – who by the way was the reason he got sentenced ta hang in the first place.

He could feel a headache comin' on.

On the other hand, if they went back to Houston, would the sheriff back there believe this caca-mammy story? Probably not; he didn't seem much of a lawman in the first place and Hammershield would browbeat Sugarbaker and he'd be right back in jail again.

And, if he could somehow get them back to Austin where the whole mess began, Judge Tyson would twist things around and involve him in the murder of the driver and guards and sentence him all over again.

Clay wondered how he got himself into this mess. He dropped what was left of the cigarillo onto the siding and ground it out with the heel of his boot.

Emma sidled up next to him and said, "You know, ta save time we could line'um up out here and form us ah firin' squad. And that would be the end of it."

Clay found it hard to believe, with the calmness of someone who had not a worry in the world, Emma had just condemned Hammershield and his men to death.

Then, he remembered how he felt about Martha, and how Emma must feel about what was done to her mother and attempted to do to her.

"Sounds like ah good plan ta me," Samuel said. "Cleans up the whole mess real nice and these good folks can be on their way."

"And what are we to do with the bodies?" Clay asked, as if he didn't already know the answer.

"I guess we just leave'um fer the varmints; although, I ain't real sure how they'd take ta eatin' skunk." Samuel said with a chuckle.

"I see," Clay said. "And after we shoot down Hammershield and his men, just how do you figure we get out of here?" he asked, waving his arms toward the wide-open space all around them.

It was Emma who came up with the answer to the question. "Why that's easy. We got us ridin' horses in one of them boxcars. We unload'um, then let the train go on its way. We brought ah horse for you, too, Mister Brentwood."

"Yeah. Pa, he thought of everthin'," Samuel said with a hint of pride.

Clay stood there, his mind in overload. While Hammershield deserved to die, he wasn't sure he was up to doing more killing.

On the other hand, he wouldn't actually have to do anything. He could hold the horses while the Andersons did the shooting.

"Ah hell," Clay said, not sure about how to handle the situation; but before he could come up with an answer, he heard a train whistle coming from back along the tracks.

"Who's that?" Samuel asked, looking at the round beam of light coming toward them.

"I don't know." Clay said, honestly. Looking toward the engineer. "You got any idea who it might be?"

The engineer scratched the back of his head and said, "There ain't another train scheduled to come through here for two more days. Your guess is as good as mine."

Clay looked up and saw Israel standing on the platform steps of the caboose, a shotgun held loosely in his hand, but ready to be brought into play at a moment's notice.

The train began to slow down, and then rolled to a stop some sixty feet behind them. A man stepped down from the engine and stood looking at them.

With the beam from the headlight shining in his eyes, it was hard for Clay to tell who had stepped from the train, but he could ascertain that it was a very short train – an engine, pulling three cars, a fuel car, a boxcar and a caboose. Strange.

Two other men stepped from the caboose and joined the man who stepped down from the engine. One of the two men was wearing a badge.

Clay dropped his hand to the butt of his pistol and waited. He wasn't sure what was goin' on, but he had to be ready for anything.

As the men advanced, the man who had stepped from the engine called out, "Clay?"

A flood of relief washed over Clay as he recognized the ranger's voice. "Bill, that you?"

When the ranger grinned and nodded his head, Clay asked, "What are you doin' here?"

"Come ta get your dumb carcass outta trouble. How are you, boy?"

Clay walked toward them, his hand stretched out. "Can't find the words ta tell ya how glad I am to see ya. Who's that you got with you?"

Howard spoke up, "It's me, your attorney, still on the job, and this here," he said pointing toward Sugarbaker, "is Ryan Sugarbaker, the marshal of Houston."

By now, they were close and Clay and Bill McDaniel were shaking hands. Clay looked at Sugarbaker and said, "I know who he is, but what is he doin' here? If he thinks he's…"

"Now just hold on a gall-darned minute," McDaniel said. "It ain't nuthin' like you're thinkin'. He knows the truth about Hammershield and he's on our side."

Clay was dumbstruck for a moment, and then he asked, "Once again, what's this all about? You and Howard, I mean."

"We've come to take you back to Austin, along with Hammershield and his gang, if we can round them up?"

Emma stepped up next to Howard and said, "Hi, I'm Emma Anderson and well, shucks, hog-tyin' them bunch ah no-goods was easier than tree'en ah coon."

Howard looked at Clay for help.

"What she means, is, her pa, her two brothers and her helped put Hammershield and his thugs in irons. They're inside that car, all tied up. Mister Anderson and his son, Israel, are watchin' them til I can figure out what ta do with'em." Clay said, pointing at the passenger car where the outlaws were being held.

"It's a long ride back to Houston and I'm looking forward to the story," Bill said, with a grin. "Let's get them relocated to the caboose."

"And then, if you gentlemen and lady," the engineer said, "don't mind, I'd like to get my passengers to Fort Worth. I'm nearly an hour late as it is."

Clay walked over and laid a hand on the engineer's shoulder, and said, "We'll be as quick as we can."

For what they'd done, using money Howard Loring was holding for him, Clay paid for the Anderson's passage all the way back to Little Rock. They tried to say no, but in the end, Clay won out. And as Clay stepped off the bottom step, Emma ran up to him and kissed him on the cheek. "If you're ever up our way, I'd like it if'n you'd come ta supper."

Clay smiled and said, "If ever I'm up that way…"

"Brentwood!"

Clay looked up and saw Hammershield and his men being moved toward the caboose. And when he didn't say anything, Hammershield, yelled, "I'll make you a deal. You and me, a knockdown–drag-out. Right here and now. You win, we go peaceful, I win, and you turn us loose.

Bill McDaniel said, "Don't pay any attention to him, Clay. They'll go along whether they want to, or not."

As the words came out, he knew he was too late. Clay was already taking off his jacket and holster and handing them to Emma, whose eyes showed her excitement.

As Bill unlocked Hammershield's handcuffs, the outlaw grinned and said, "This shouldn't take long."

McDaniel said nothing and Howard Loring crossed his fingers.

Word quickly passed among the passengers as faces were plastered against the windows of the train to see what was going to happen. The engineer, who had been chewing at the bit to be on his way, delayed leaving so he could witness the fight. He figured a story like this could get free beer at the watering holes in Fort Worth.

Hammershield took off his coat and handed it to one of his men, then turned and walked toward Clay, expecting to make this a short fight.

Aaron Hammershield felt confident that his experience as a professional fighter back east would make whipping this country clod an easy exercise, but what he didn't know was, not only was Clay an experienced rough and tumble street fighter, raised in Southeastern Kansas, where if you couldn't defend yourself, you spent a lot of time in hiding and he wasn't' much at hiding. And by the time he reached his sixteenth birthday, he'd also done a bit of boxing in and around Wichita and had an undefeated record.

As they circled each other, Clay watched Hammershield closely, noting the way he moved and realized Hammershield for what he was, an experienced boxer. But was he a street fighter, Clay wondered? That he would know shortly.

"Get him!" Emma shouted.

That slight distraction was the opening Hammershield was looking for and he sent a left to Clay's jaw and followed with a hard uppercut to Clay's chin, which sent Clay stumbling backward onto his back.

"Get up, Brentwood, I'm not through with you, yet," Hammershield yelled.

Clay shook his head to clear the flashing lights and slowly got to his feet. "Can't let that happen too many times," he muttered to himself. And, I hope Emma keeps her trap shut, he thought, but didn't say out loud.

Once again, they circled each other, each looking for an opening. Hammershield, feeling over confident, feinted with a left and sent a right hook towards Clay's jaw. Clay threw up his left and blocked the right hook, then sent his right fist into Hammershield's stomach, doubling him over and causing air to rush out of his mouth. Before the man could recover, Clay sent a left hook to the side of Hammershield's head, sending him to the ground. Clay was tempted to kick him in the head and end it but decided against it.

When Hammershield regained his feet, his eyes were blazing daggers at Clay, but he'd lost some of his cockiness. Instead, his blood ran hot and he wanted to kill this man with his fists; beat him to death.

As they circled, Hammershield said, "Better start praying, smart guy. You're about to meet your maker," and started for Clay.

With unexpected quickness, Clay met Hammershield head on, throwing lefts and rights to both the man's face and body - blow after blow without any let-up, until the outlaw staggered around, unable to even raise his hands. Clay decided it was time to finish it and delivered the final blow, a right cross to the temple area that came with all the force Clay could muster.

Hammershield's head was knocked to the side, dragging his body with it and the outlaw went down, out cold, his unseeing eyes staring at the sky.

Except for the hissing of the train engines, the night air was quiet. Everyone just stood there in awe. They were amazed that after being knocked down, Clay had taken control of the fight so quickly, and put Hammershield flat of his back, out for the count.

Bill McDaniel looked at Clay with new respect as he walked over and looked down at Hammershield. The man's face was swollen, black and blue, and blood had gushed from his nose, staining his shirt. The professional boxer had more than met his match.

Bill McDaniel and Howard Loring pulled Hammershield to his feet. Bill slapped his face to wake him up so he could put his jacket back on before they handcuffed him, Bill looked at Howard and said, "Remind me to never challenge Clay to a fistfight."

"Only if you'll do the same for me," Howard said with a grin.

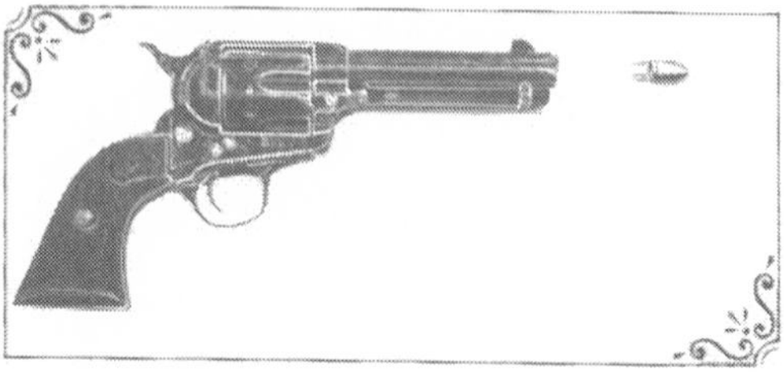

# CHAPTER TWENTY-ONE

While all this was going on, other things were happening back in Austin. Word about Abigail and Judge Tyson had gotten to the ears of the women in town and Abigail had not only lost her position as Sunday school teacher, but the Ladies League of Austin held a special session and decided Abigail Schuster was not the kind they wanted in Austin. Together, they marched down to Abigail's home and told her, in no uncertain terms, that she would no longer be welcome in Austin, and suggested she leave town and find residence elsewhere.

Abigail Schuster was mortified and told the old biddies they could have Austin and all the sinful hypocrites who lived there. She told them she would leave just as soon as she could sell her house.

The male members of the city council, husbands of the women of the Ladies League, after much berating by their wives, decided the city should buy Abigail's house and turn it into a hospital, of sorts.

Three days after Judge Tyson left Austin, Texas, and headed for Denver, Miss Abigail Schuster boarded a train and headed for the same city, far to the north, not unhappy to be leaving this sinful den of inequity. She would soon be with her beloved Horatio and they could begin a new life together. And, she would hear his reason for borrowing a thousand dollars of her money without asking. She assured herself that he would have a legitimate reason.

The dining car was not yet full when she ordered a cup of tea and laced it with whiskey from a flask she carried in her purse. She silently toasted a new beginning – a new life with Horatio. She wished the train would go faster.

Judge Horatio B. Tyson was sitting in the dining car of the train, enjoying a glass of whiskey and his freedom from that dreadful town and the pursuits of Abigail Schuster. He patted the wallet resting in the inside pocket of his coat and said, "For this and the other pleasures you gave me, I thank you Abigail, but all things must come to an end."

When the porter brought him his second drink, he asked, "How much longer before we get to Denver?"

The porter looked at his watch and said, "Not too much longer. It's just past six and we should get into Denver sometime around mid-night, sir."

Horatio paid for his drink and added a substantial tip.

The porter smiled and said, "Thank you, sir," as he accepted the money.

Just then, the train lurched to a stop, sending dishes and glasses onto the floor.

"What's happening?" the judge asked.

"Oh lordy, looks like we bein' robbed, again. Third time this month."

Horatio, not wanting to be robbed of his money, raced to his stateroom and locked himself inside.

He was sitting on the couch with a single shot derringer pistol in his hand when the door came flying open and he saw a man wearing a scarf tied across his face and a gun in his hand. Without any qualms, Horatio fired at the intruder and watched the front of the man's shirt turn red as he stumbled back into the passageway.

Then, before he could reload, two other bandits rushed in and grabbed him, and after taking his money, they dragged him off the train and threw him down onto the ground in front of a man who was obviously the leader of the gang.

After they explained what Horatio had done, the leader of the gang walked over and kicked Horatio between the legs, causing him to throw-up. Then with slowness and deliberation, the man circled Horatio, kicking him in all the vital parts of his body.

When Horatio finally came back to reality, he looked around and saw that both, the train and the outlaws were gone, and in their place, six Indians with painted faces, were sitting on their horses, staring down at him.

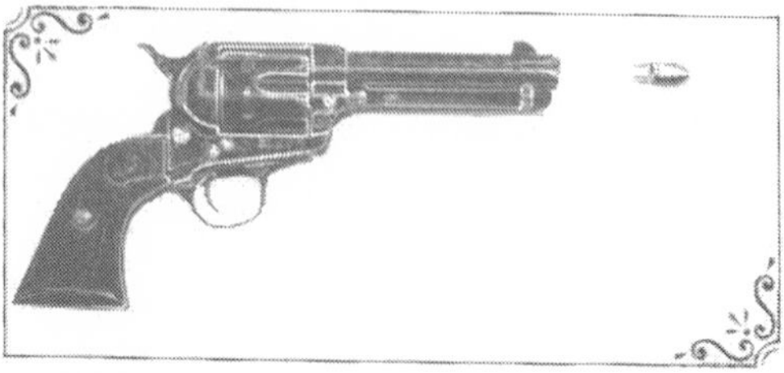

# CHAPTER TWENTY-TWO

The trip back to Austin was long and tedious. First, they'd stopped in Houston to return the train. The engineer seemed to be sad the experience was over, but glad he'd gotten a chance to see what his engine would do, and walked around, shaking each man's hand.

The marshal also thanked them for the experience. It was something he'd never forget, he'd told them. While shaking Clay's hand, he said, "I'm real sorry about the way I treated you, Mister Brentwood. Seems I was a mite gullible. But in my defense, I've not had much experience at such things. You see, I only took this job because my cousin, who was the marshal here in Austin at the time, got layed up. And well, he asked me to take his place. He told me Houston was a quiet town and nothing ever happened."

That brought a laugh and Sugarbaker's face turned a bright pink.

The following morning, after a good breakfast, they stepped into their saddles and headed west, leading Hammershield and his men, tied to their horse and a lead rope between each horse, along with a packhorse with what they'd need for the trip.

The ride back to Austin took them three days, and during that time, Clay and Bill McDaniel had time to talk. McDaniel explained about how he and Howard had gotten rid of Judge Tyson, along with their talk with the governor, explaining to him about Abigail and the judge. Howard was quick to notice that the ranger left out the part about what he'd suggested Clay's new sentence would be.

"So, I'm gonna have ta stand trial all over, again?" Clay asked.

"Yes, but it will be with a new, hopefully unbiased judge," Howard said. "And the fact that you helped apprehend Hammershield and his gang, should go a long way in showing the judge that you are not some maniac who goes around murdering people for no reason."

Clay agreed to go back and face a new trial because he didn't want to be a fugitive on the run for the rest of his life.

A day before Clay arrived back in Austin, to face a new judge, Abigail Schuster's train pulled into the Denver terminal. She carried a suitcase that contained not only a few clothes, but also the money from the sale of her house and the other cash she had stored in drawers and cupboards around the place, which amounted to a little over, nine thousand dollars.

She walked out to the front of the train station and looked around, marveling at the sight of the famous city.

At first, she was going to hire a hansom to take her to a hotel but changed her mind and decided to walk. The weather was nice, even if it was late afternoon. And she was sure there would be a nice hotel nearby.

She strolled along the sidewalk, looking into the windows of the stores admiring all there was to see. She and Horatio would fit in here nicely, she thought to herself.

In the distance, she saw a sign that said, HOTEL. She smiled and headed for it, anxious to get a bath and have something to eat. She'd gone only half a block when she passed an alleyway. Not being from the city, she paid scant attention.

Out of nowhere, a hand grabbed her and jerked her into the darkness. She couldn't see her attacker, but his breath smelled of liquor and his dirty hand covered her mouth so she couldn't scream. Her eyes were wild with fright and she squirmed in an effort to get away. Her attacker lost his grip and as she turned to face him, the last thing Abigail Schuster ever saw was the large knife blade, plunging toward her chest.

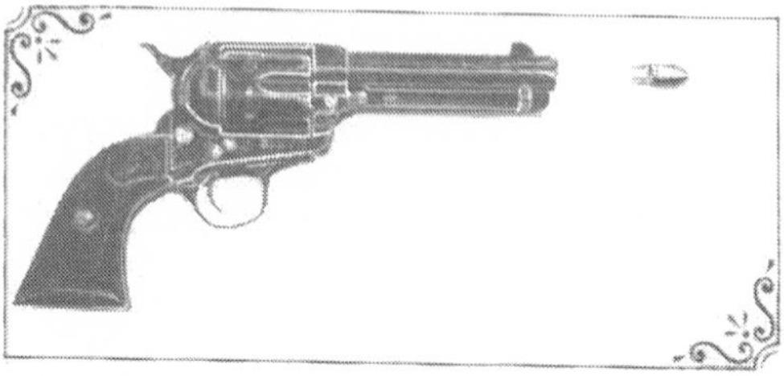

# CHAPTER TWENTY-THREE

It was late afternoon of the third day when they reached the outskirts of Austin, and Bill McDaniel pulled them to a stop. He stepped down from his saddle and rubbed his sore back. He waited until Clay and Howard had dismounted before telling the prisoners to stay on their horses.

McDaniel walked over to Clay and said in a low voice, "I'm sorry about this, but I have to put you in cuffs before we get to town. Bringing you in needs to look official. You understand, don't ya?"

Clay took his time before committing himself to the ranger. First, he looked Bill in the eyes and saw real concern, then turned his head and looked at his attorney.

Howard gave a slight smile and shrugged his shoulders. "It's going to be alright," he said.

Clay figured after everything he'd been through and them not givin' up on him, he'd give it one more try. He wanted this to be over with and be a free man again.

They rode into Austin with Bill McDaniel in the lead; Clay followed him with a rope tied to the ranger's saddle horn. Behind Clay, with a rope tied to his saddle horn, was Hammershield and his gang, strung out in single file, all tied together. With a rifle across his lap, Howard brought up the rear.

After taking Hammershield and his men to the city jail and locking them in, Bill returned to where Clay and Howard sat their horses.

"For appearances", Bill had said as he took Clay back to the same jailhouse he'd been in before, only this time the guards were all different and treated him like a human being.

Howard explained that after talking with the governor, the governor had made a lot of changes, like all new guards at the jailhouse and he personally appointed a new judge; one he knew from back in St. Louis, by the name of, Archibald P. Webster. I haven't met him yet, but I've been assured he is a fair and impartial man.

"When does the new trial begin?" Clay asked.

Howard shook his head. "Not sure yet. Bill and I are meeting with the judge in the morning. We're hoping it will be no more than a few days."

"Me too," Clay said. "I'm none too fond of jail time and I've sure been doin' my fair share of it lately."

Howard laid his hand on Clay's shoulder and said, "I have a feeling things are going to work out a lot different, this time."

"Does that mean you think this new judge will set me free?"

Howard Loring wanted to open up and tell Clay everything, but he couldn't. He'd promised Bill to keep his mouth shut. And even if he didn't agree completely, he didn't want to spoil the ranger's fun.

Not wanting to out and out lie to Clay, he said, "I can't tell you what the judge will do. That will remain his decision."

Clay gave a sigh and Howard spoke up. "Don't look so worried. With you helping capture Hammershield, and coming back, voluntarily - that should say a lot about your character. As for the other, by the letter of the law thing…"

"I know, I know," Clay said. "But not hangin', this time, right?"

Howard smiled as he dropped his hand from Clay's shoulder. "No, I'm confident there will be no hanging this time."

Back in his cell, Clay thought about their conversation and the look in his lawyer's eyes. "He knows more than he's sayin'. I'd bet ah plug nickel on that," he said.

"What's that? You need somethin'?" the guard asked.

"No, I was just talkin' to myself, tryin' ta get things straight in my head," Clay said with a grin.

"I understand you're the one who rode into Bristol Springs and took care of the Beeler gang," the guard said.

Clay looked up, surprised. "Does everybody in the whole world know about it?" he asked.

"Didn't mean it that way," the guard said. "I got ah cousin that lives in Bristol Springs and he wrote me ah letter about it just after it happened. Then I heard about you being here and the sentence that other judge give you. Didn't seem fair to me. And now, here you are again."

Clay smiled and nodded his head. "Yeah, here I am, again."

"Sure hope this judge does ah better job than that other one did."

"Thank you. So do I."

"I gotta go, but if you need anything, anything at all, you just give ah holler. Name's Riley.

The next day during lunch, Clay's attorney came by and told him what the judge had decided to do. "The judge has decided to handle the Hammershield and his men's case, first. He said he wants to give your case some more thought; wants to review all the facts, since neither Abigail or Judge Tyson are available to testify, he has only the court reports."

Clay gave out with a long sigh, but before he could protest, Howard went on.

"Now here's the good part. He said he'd read your transcript twice and wasn't too keen on the sentence you were given. He agreed that by the letter of the law, you need to be punished for taking the law into your own hands, but thought hanging was a bit severe. He figures Judge Tyson was being manipulated by Abigail Schuster, which we all know was true."

"What does all of this mean?" Clay asked. "What kind of sentence is he gonna give me, life in prison? Not sure I wouldn't rather hang and get it over with."

"I can't say what he'll do," Howard said, still not lying, but not telling all he knew, either. "But I can tell you that I have a good feeling about this judge."

"Well at least that's somethin', I guess," Clay said. "Oh yeah, thanks for the book about Black Beard, the pirate. These outlaws today have nuthin' on him, do they?"

Howard grinned. "I thought you might find that interesting. I can bring you more if you want me to."

Clay raised his hands, palms forward. "Whoa. No more! I ain't plannin' on stayin' in here too much longer, unless you know somethin' I don't."

"Sorry, I didn't mean it that way. Of course, I'm sure it won't be but a few more days. The judge wants to dispose of the Hammershield case as quickly as possible. Their court date is set for Monday, which is only two days from now."

Well, it can't be too soon for me. I wanna know somethin' one way or another," Clay said with a bit of apprehension in his voice.

They made their goodbyes with the promise of visits with any news that came up.

When Clay was ushered to his cell, he found a stack of newspapers and dime novels stacked near his bunk. He looked back over his shoulder and saw Riley grinning like the cat that ate the canary.

"Thanks," he said and watched as Riley turned and strutted back to the guard station.

Sitting on his bunk, he leaned back and let random thoughts come and go as they may. Was this the life he had to look forward to, sittin' on ah bunk, readin' dime novels, or would he spend the rest of his life breakin' rock with ah sledgehammer? He'd known what the consequences of his actions might be, but he was holding too much anger in him at the time. Curly Beeler and his bunch deserved ta die for what they did to him and all the others, too. Couldn't ah judge see that? He didn't want to die, but he didn't want ta spend the rest of his life behind prison walls, either.

Clay didn't know how long he'd been sittin' there but when he heard his name called out he looked toward the cell door. Riley was escorting the woman from the restaurant and she was bringing his dinner.

She walked in and sat the tray on the small table that had been added since his last visit here. She smiled and said, "You still have credit from the money the senora left so you will be getting your dinners again."

Clay wasn't sure what to say, so he just said, "Thanks."

Clay watched in appreciation as her skirt swished this way and that as she left his cell. He figured her to be in her mid-thirties, and a fetchin' woman, with long dark hair and big blue eyes, with just a sprinkle of freckles across her nose. And she has some of the whitest, and straightest teeth he'd ever seen.

When she'd gone, Clay sat down in the only chair and pulled the cloth off his dinner and smiled. There was a good-sized steak, fried potatoes, a bowl of beans, tortillas, coffee and a big slice of apple pie.

He looked toward Riley who was standing there, grinnin' like a young boy who'd just pulled off a big prank.

"Bein' in jail might not be so bad, after all," Clay said.

"Specially if a woman like that brings his dinner ever day," he said using his hands to make the sign of an hourglass.

The dinner was the best food he'd had in some time. And that night, for the first time in weeks, he slept like he was at peace with the world.

The weekend was spent resting and reading and talking with Riley who seemed a pleasant sort. He was of Irish decent and had come to America three years ago with his wife, who passed away giving birth to an unborn child. He'd held a lot of odd jobs, just tryin' to get over his grief and was headed to Bristol Springs to meet up with his cousin when he landed in Austin. He'd been drivin' ah wagon loaded with furniture, from St. Louis, Missouri to Austin for ah family who had moved recently here. After collectin' his pay, he was sittin' in the saloon, havin' ah few pints, when he was offered another drivin' job, this time to Houston and back. He told Clay he'd worked that job for over a year when he heard about this job and jumped at the chance. The work was easy and the pay was good. He would save some money, then go out to Bristol Springs and buy into his cousin's business.

"And what business is that?" Clay inquired.

"He's in the mercantile business, has his own store, he does. Can you imagine me, part owner in ah dry goods store?"

"Yes, I can," Clay, said with a grin. "By the way, your' cousin's name wouldn't happen ta be, Ned Baker, would it?"

Riley shook his head and grinned, "Shur and begora, ain't he the one who wrote me about you, now, he was. Aye, and it's him I'll be ah goin' inta business with."

"Well, I don't see how you could do better, he's ah fine man," Clay said.

"Well now, that's good ta know because the actual truth is, I ain't never met the man; just know him through another relative back in Ireland and ah few letters."

Monday dawned with dark clouds and rain. Clay was looking out of the window of his cell and saw Hammershield and his gang bein' lead across to the courthouse. He watched until they disappeared in the side door, then turned his attention to the front of the courthouse, where he saw people hurrying up the steps.

He turned back from the window and walked back over and sat down at his small table. He picked up a newspaper and read an article about a young outlaw by the name of Billy the Kid.

Clay had just finished his supper of beef stew with a whole pan of cornbread and a large slab of rhubarb pie. He was sipping on his coffee when Riley yelled out, "Your lawyer is here, want ta see'em?"

"Sure, send him in. And do you think it's possible to get another chair for him ta sit on?"

"One lawyer and one chair, comin' up," Riley said as he hurried back toward the guardroom, chuckling to himself at his joke.

After Riley had gone, Howard and Clay sat looking at each other. "Well?" Clay finally asked.

Howard nodded his head up and down. "I like this man. He's very methodical and he wants to see you in court tomorrow morning, first thing."

"Me? Why does he want to see me? I thought it was Hammershield and his bunch who's on trial."

Howard nodded his head, again and said, "He wants you there as a witness. You saw him shoot Jake Comers and Julio Flores, didn't you?"

"Yeah, but…"

"It will be another feather in your cap when you go before him with your case," Howard said with conviction.

The next morning, Clay was taken to the courtroom, this time with just handcuffs and not in shackles. He'd had a bath and a shave and wore clean clothes.

Clay studied the judge and liked what he saw. He was a portly man who carried his weight well. He stood around five feet ten inches and had thinning hair, which at one time was auburn, but now laced with gray. He looked at Clay and nodded, studying the man who was to be his next case.

Clay was led to the witness chair, sworn in and took his seat. The judge looked down at him and explained why he was here, and for the next twenty minutes Clay told his story, leaving nothing out, as Howard had instructed him to do.

"And do you see the men who killed the prison driver and two guards?" the judge asked.

"Yes," Clay said.

"Are they in the courtroom today?"

"Yes," Clay said, again.

"Would you be so kind, Mister Brentwood, to point them out to the court?"

Clay pointed toward the men in Hammershield's gang.

"You're sure these were the men? You have no doubt?" the judge asked.

"Yes sir, I'm sure and I have no doubts. I saw them do it."

"And you say you were holding the reins of their horses at the time. Were you a member of their gang?"

"I was holding the reins of their horses only because the Kiowa, that's the man with the long black hair with the feather in it," Clay said, pointing at the Indian, who was staring daggers at him, "had a knife stuck against my ribs at the time. And no sir, at no time was I ever a part of their gang."

One more question, Mister Brentwood. Will you tell us about the murder of Jake Comers and Julio Flores."

Clay took his time and described what happened and what Hammershield had said.

When he was finished, the judge looked at the county prosecutor and asked, "Do you have any questions, Mister Prosecutor?"

The man lowered his head, shaking it. "No questions, your honor."

The judge turned his attention back to Clay, and asked, "Mister Brentwood, were you promised any favors for testifying today? Anything at all pertaining to your case?"

"No sir. I was just told by my lawyer that I was to testify what I know about Aaron Hammershield and his men while I was their captive. That's all."

"Thank you," the judge said, then looked at Riley, who was seated on the far side of the courtroom.

"Mister Riley, you may take the prisoner back to his cell. And thank you again for your time and testimony, Mister Brentwood. You've served the court well, today," he said turning to look at Clay, who just nodded his head and stood up.

Clay had been back to his cell a little over an hour when Howard showed up, grinning from ear to ear. "You did good. The judge was impressed, but you sure made an enemy of Hammershield. He told the judge you were lying to save your own skin, but the judge saw right through it and sentenced them all to be sent to Huntsville and hung."

Clay didn't say anything. He just stared at his attorney, remembering receiving the same sentence.

“Finally, coming back to reality, he asked, “Did he say when he’ll hear my case?” Clay wanted to get it over with.

“Wednesday,” Howard said. “Tomorrow, he wants to take the day off and go fishing. Said it helps him get things straight in his mind.”

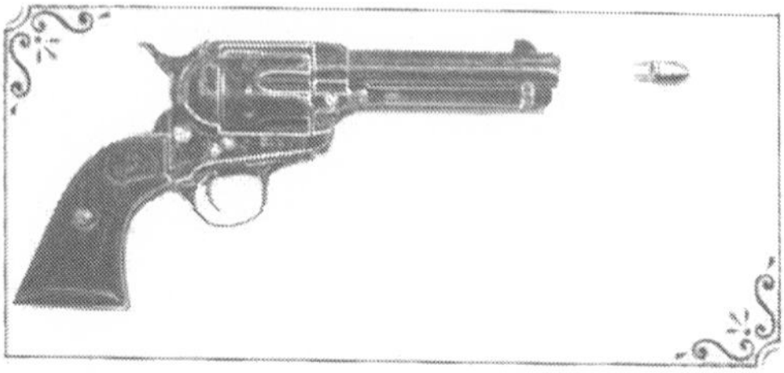

# CHAPTER TWENTY-FOUR

Once again, the courtroom was packed. There were people standing along the back wall. Clay shook his head. Didn't these people have jobs to go to? Most of them had already been here for his first trial. He just didn't understand the attraction. Sighing, he took his seat next to Howard who assured him everything would turn out alright.

They stood up when the judge came in and took his seat. After adjusting some papers, he looked down at Howard and Clay, and said, "This is the second hearing on the same case; one that has been ruled on by another judge. But, since there seems to be some question about his ruling, the governor has asked me to take a second look at the case, and either agree with the first ruling, or, draw my own conclusions."

The judge looked directly at Clay and asked, "Do you understand what's going on here, Mister Brentwood?"

Clay stood up and said, "Yes, your honor."

"Good," the judge said. "Now, let us proceed. Mister Brentwood, please come forward and get sworn in."

Clay stood up and walked up to the bailiff and raised his right hand and swore to tell the truth, the whole truth and nothing but the truth, then mounted the witness stand and sat down.

The judge looked down at Clay and said; "You do understand this will not be like the first time, where there was a prosecuting attorney and witnesses against you. I will listen to your story and based on what I've read and what I hear today, will render my decision."

Clay looked up at the judge and said, "Yes sir."

The judge smiled and said, "And you do understand that the decision I make here today, will be the final one. There will be no appeals."

Clay, still looking up at the judge, said, "Yes sir."

The judge nodded and looked out over the packed courtroom and said, "This is the second trial of Clay Brentwood versus Abigail Schuster, whereas Mister Brentwood is accused of murdering her brother, Charles "Curly" Beeler. Court is now in session."

Let the record show this case will be judged on past testimony, along with the testimony presented here today by Mister Brentwood."

Turning back to Clay, the judge said, "I know you've already told your story, or at least part of it before, but I haven't heard it and I need to before rendering my decision. So, if you will, Mister Brentwood, tell us your side and do be complete, leave nothing out."

Clay cleared his throat and this time was able to tell his story completely without any interruptions; even the part about him trying to see the sheriff first but finding out Curly had shot him four days earlier and taken over the town. He went on to describe what happened as he came out of the barn. They had started the dance, not him. But in the end, he did admit that when it came to Curly, he had killed him for what he had done to his wife and unborn child.

When he finished, the courtroom was as quiet as a graveyard; you couldn't even hear people breathing.

Finally, the judge rapped his gavel and said, "The court will take a two-hour recess to consider this case. The defendant and his lawyer will be back in this courtroom at one o'clock to hear my decision."

He rapped his gavel again, and said, "Court is adjourned until one o'clock."

When the judge had disappeared back into his chambers, Clay stood up and looked at his attorney.

Since Clay was dressed in his own clothes and not wearing any restraints, Riley agreed with Howard that they should all go to the restaurant for lunch instead of taking Clay back to his cell.

Bill McDaniel had been sitting at the back of the courtroom and was invited to join them.

Clay was enjoying his freedom, such as it was, and wondered if this was the last time he would be free?

Most of the discussion was about Hammershield and his men. McDaniel said the Chief of Police here in Austin had taken it upon himself to appoint a special guard unit to escort them to Huntsville. There would be two guards riding several hundred feet in front, checking for a possible ambush. The prison wagon would have a driver and two guards, armed to the teeth. And there would be two more guards riding on horses some two hundred feet behind, in case there was an attack from behind.

Several people who had been in the courtroom stopped by to wish Clay well, telling him how touched they were by his story.

They had just finished eating and were about to leave, when all hell broke loose. Several loud explosions filled the air and rattled the dishes in the restaurant. They ran into the street just in time to see Hammershield and his men escaping through three holes in the side of the jail. There was a man there with horses and the outlaws jumped aboard and started racing away.

McDaniel stepped into the street, drew his pistol, took careful aim and pulled the trigger. The big forty-four roared and an instant later, one of the outlaws was knocked from his horse, while the others disappeared down the street.

The Chief of Police ran out of the jailhouse and saw the dead man lying in the middle of the street, then looked toward Bill. They nodded to one another, then Bill, Clay, Riley and Howard hurried toward the courthouse. It was ten minutes to one.

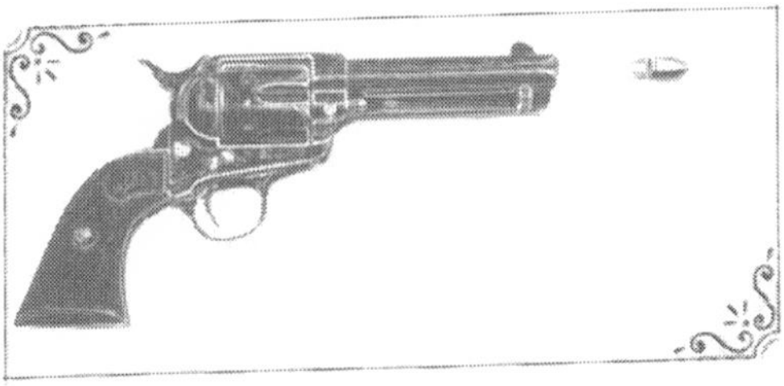

# CHAPTER TWENTY-FIVE

As soon as they entered the courthouse, McDaniel headed for the judge's chambers to explain what happened, while Riley, Clay and Howard went to their seats in the court-room.

The place was already crowded. People were talking about the escape and the man who'd been shot from his horse by the Texas Ranger.

Shortly, the bailiff called for quiet just before the judge entered the courtroom and took his seat and stared out across the room. Finally, he said, "These are tough times we live in where the criminal seems to think he can do as he pleases. And because of our shortage of officers, many times they get away with it; such as what happened a few minutes ago."

The people sat in silence, waiting to hear what else the judge had to say, and after what seemed an eternity, he said, "The court is now ready to render its decision in the case of Clay Brentwood. Please stand and face me, Mister Brentwood."

Bill McDaniel had entered the courtroom and was sitting just behind Clay, and along with Howard Loring, he stood up when Clay did.

For some reason, Clay wasn't nervous. His friends were standing next to him and he felt the judge would be fair in his sentence. He just hoped it wouldn't be life in prison.

"Mister Brentwood," the judge said, "The court has read the evidence against you and has listened to your side. And based upon your actions in helping capture Aaron Hammershield and his gang of ruffians, the court has taken that into consideration. The court also takes into consideration the circumstances for which you felt obligated to hunt down Curly and his gang in order to keep a promise to your dead wife. And based on the fact that you tried to get in touch with the local sheriff, shows the court that you are not a hardened killer. But, even so, choosing to take the law into your own hands cannot go unpunished."

The judge took a break in his speech and took a sip of water.

"Now, as to your sentence. I have given it much thought and have decided that sitting in a prison would be a waste of time and the money it takes to keep you. Instead, I have decided community service will be in the best interest of the people."

The room was suddenly abuzz with whispers. The bailiff called out, "Quiet in the court!" When the room settled down, the judge continued. "It is therefore the order of this court that you, Clay Brentwood, shall spend the next two years in the service of the Texas Rangers, overseen by the chief of the rangers, Mister William McDaniel."

Clay was speechless and just stood there, feeling slaps on his back. Somewhere in the distance, he heard the judge's gavel rap and heard him say, "Court adjourned,"

He was finally jerked back to reality when he heard McDaniel say, "Com'on ranger, we need to get you over to the office and sworn in. I need to give you your first assignment. You're goin' after Hammershield and I expect results."

As they walked out of the courthouse and headed for the office of the Texas Rangers, Clay looked over at McDaniel and said, “Two years under you, as a Texas Ranger… Did I hear that right?”

“That’s right,” McDaniel said with a grin. “And it ain’t gonna be no picnic, either.”

Clay grinned and said; “Now that’s what I call, unjust punishment.”

THE END

## MEET THE AUTHOR

JARED McVAY is a four-time award-winning author. He writes several genres, including - westerns, fantasy, action/adventure, and children's books. Before becoming an author, he was a professional actor on stage, in movies and on television. As a young man he was a cowboy, a rodeo clown, a lumberjack, a power lineman, a world-class sailor and spent his military time with the Navy Sea Bees where he learned his electrical trade. When not writing you can find him fishing somewhere or traveling around and just enjoying life with his girlfriend, Jerri.

# THANK YOU FOR READING!

If you enjoyed this book, we would appreciate your customer review on your book seller's website or on Goodreads.

Also, we would like for you to know that you can find more great books like this one at

**www.SixGunBooks.com**

Stories so real you can smell the gunsmoke.™

SIX
GUN
BOOKS™